When She's Bad, I'm Badder: 3

Jiao & Dreek, A Crazy Love Story

I want to give a special thanks to each and every one of my readers who've been rocking with me from the very beginning and all the new ones. Please don't be mad if you don't see your name. (I had to use your FB names.) I tried to remember all of you but it's so many of you. ☐

Candiance Noble, Sommer Terell, Sophia Sophia, Jonnika Williams, Courtney Brownlee, Angel Perez, Chanell Cohen, Taylor Kirk, Denica Freeman, Badja Johnson, Qiana Bray, Denashia Smith, Dorether Singletary, Allanah Singletary, Zatashia White, Tootie Williams, Kashauna Howard, Latanya Gilliard, Marisol Gomez, Tina Padilla, Jennifer Singleton, Shanta Herrera, Nette Jack, Sweets Gray, Marquitta Jones, Lakeetha Reece, Adrienne Martin, Regina Boykin, Regina Jefferson Rudolph, Yvette McCray, Tanya Simmons, Kea-Juanna Brantley, Kadeene Smith, Jessica Jessica Hudson, Cheryl Simmons, Donna Ross, Jaime Knight, Kendra Williams, Jewel Ann Jew-Jew Sayers Harmon, Felicia Nelson, Felicia Darklovely, Alesia Goolsby, Chanice NeNe Wilson, Ashley LeNae, BeBe Mon'e, Neish Johnson, Dominque Acklin,

Cynthia Daniels, Danie Marie, Evonne Dozier, Zavia Stewart, Toni Zardies, Viola King (You are always in my prayers) Sadie Boopie Crooks, Dawn Gilley, Kiesha Reams, Theresa Ann, Derrika Simms, Staci West, Iris Freeman, Wendy Slaughter Williams, Amanda Schmidt, Ginette Tambwe, Tatina Wilson, LeMecia Williams, Deborah Holden, Jeanette Thurman, Neish Johnson, LaKeisha Day, Shameeka James, Erica Alwaysdoingme Banks, Thiland Barlow, Tee Carter and many others.

And to all the authors, publishers and supporters, I appreciate each and every one of you too. It's way too many of you to name but I see you.

*Previously…*

## Jiao

"Who do he think he is not calling me? Where could he be? I mean we weren't arguing or anything so I don't understand." I paced back and forth talking on the phone to Sommer.

"Sis, calm down. You're getting worked up and it's probably something to with their business in Cuba." I thought about what she said and I remember Dreek saying sometimes they would up and leave the country with no notice.

"Fuck this. I'm going to look for him."

"Where are you going to look fool? You have no idea where to even start."

"Bitch, I'm going to Queenie's and try to figure out where the bitch Mandy lives. I swear if he's over either of their house, I'm fucking killing him."

"Bring my nephew here before you go off and do something stupid."

"His nana is here and she just put him down for a nap. I'll call you when I hear something.

"Bitch, come get me then."

"Who's going to keep an eye on Raven?"

"The nanny. I'll be ready when you get here."

I hung up, ran in my room and threw on a sweat suit. I laced up my brand new peach and white air macs, grabbed my keys, phone and ran down the steps. I looked in the living room and Dree was lying on the couch watching cartoons as usual.

 I thought about going in the room we had for Dreek's mom here and check on my son, but then she'll question the shit out of me. I don't need to hear her tell me not to lay hands on him either. I could never agree to it anyway; especially if he is with another chick.

I blew the horn in front of Sommer's house and she came out wearing an all black sweat suit with all black sneakers. At first, I was going to question her but changed my mind because she's my ride or die, so she's supposed to be ready for war. She put her finger up when she got in the truck and told me to be quiet. It sounded like she was talking to Percy.

I took the hour drive over to Queenie's and scanned the parking lot. I was mad as hell because Dreek had us living far away and now it would take me longer to find him.

I had Sommer call her dad and ask if he could find Mandy's information out. At first, he said no, but then she called Susie, who called us back and gave it to us. She said Sommer's dad made her promise he could spend time with her if he gave it to her. Susie planned on taking him back once she found out the truth about Charlotte but said he had to suffer first.

"Pull over J." Sommer pointed to a gas station.

"For what? My tank is good."

"Charlotte is there and I want to see who she's with." She pointed again and sure enough, Charlotte came out the store and walked to a car with tinted windows.

"Follow the car." I snapped my neck.

"Bitch, Dreek ain't going nowhere." I sucked my teeth and did like she asked. The car drove to the projects and stopped. Both doors opened and you wouldn't believe who the fuck stepped out with her.

"What you want to do?"

"Let's find Dreek and we'll come back here another time."

"Sommer, I think we should deal with this now. What if they're not around when we return?"

"Oh, they'll be around. If they wanted to run, they would have. There's something here they want, and neither of them will leave town until they have it. We just have to figure out what it is." I pulled off and we were in route to my old best friends house.

"Bitch, there's no cars in the driveway. You think Mandy is here?" Sommer asked when we stepped out the truck.

"I need to make sure."

"OPEN THIS DOOR BITCH." I yelled out as I banged on it. I didn't care who the fuck heard me.

"DREEK, I SWEAR TO GOD IF YOU'RE IN THERE YOU BETTER SAY GOODBYE TO YOUR KIDS. I

PROMISE YOU, I HAVE A BULLET FOR YOU." The more I yelled, the angrier I got. No one came to the door, so I kicked a window out and climbed in. Call me crazy all you want but a bitch had to be 100 percent sure he wasn't in here.

I opened the door for Sommer and made my way around Mandy's place. She had a decent spot and it the decorating wasn't bad. There was a unique smell in here, and only one person I know wears this type of cologne and it damn sure isn't Dreek. *When the fuck did he come here and is he looking for me?* I felt myself trembling and before I could turn the knob to the other bedroom, Sommer asked if I were ok. Instead of going in, I turned around and told her we had to leave.

"He's here."

"Who?" I raised my eyebrows.

"Bitch, I don't know what that means. Who the fuck is here because Dreek damn sure ain't?" I ignored her. I forgot no one knew about him, not even her. In due time, I will find that motherfucker but right now, my focus is on my so called man.

"Where else could they be? Didn't you say they had a warehouse?"

"Oh shit, that's right. I was so into following Charlotte I forgot to tell you. When Percy and I were talking, I heard Dreek in the background saying he had to put in some new orders before they get on the plane. They have to be there and if not, then they just left to go to Cuba."

"Orders. What the hell is that about?"

"I don't know but it's time to find out what Charlotte said Percy had hiding in the warehouse anyway." I forgot Charlotte's messy ass said that to her. We pulled on the dark street where the warehouse was and stepped out the car. It was quiet as hell out and all you could hear were crickets.

"Hello Jiao." I froze when I heard his voice. Sommer looked at him and then gave me a confusing stare. Why the fuck didn't we check our surroundings first?

"Long time no see baby." He licked his lips.

"The baby did your body real, real good." My phone started ringing and it was my father. I sent him to voicemail but couldn't help but wonder why he was calling me this late.

11

"Didn't think I'd see you two bitches here." Mandy said as she stepped out the car. Here we are down the street from my man's warehouse dealing with two people I'd rather not be around.

"Bitch. I don't think the last ass whooping was enough. Shall we go again." I put my hair up.

"I miss you baby girl." He kissed my neck and I smacked the shit out of him.

"Is that the way to treat the man who's going to kill your son's father and whisk you away to live the good life?"

"What do you want?" I stood there staring at him. Mandy had a big ass grin on her face.

"Who I want is standing behind you?" I turned around and there stood Dreek, Percy, Jaime, Robert and a shitload of other niggas. Dreek looked as if he were injured but I couldn't be certain. I did see what looks like a bandage under his shirt and the more he walked up on me, I noticed a slight limp.

"Somebody better tell me right now how you two know each other." The anger spoke volumes in Dreek's voice.

"Your baby daddy is going to kill you." Mandy pointed to my shirt. There sat a red dot on my chest. Sommer moved me out the way but the dot was everywhere I was. Why wasn't there a red dot on Sommer? Was he watching us from inside?

"Do you want to tell him my love, or should I?" He had a smug grin on his face.

"Oooh, let me tell it." Mandy said jumping up and down like a fucking kid.

"Dreek, this is my cousin Hector and you see." She walked up to me and stood in my face.

"Hector and Jiao were a couple a few years back and remember when I told you your precious Jiao wasn't what she seemed? Well, here you have it." She rubbed her hands together like she was delivering some important news.

"Meet the chick who was working with Hector to take down you down." Sommer looked at me and covered her mouth and I could feel everyone's eyes on me, but the only ones mine met, were Dreek's. I saw love, sadness, hatred and most of all anger.

"Jiao no." Sommer said and Percy snatched her away from me.

"I can't save you J. You fucked up big time." Jaime said and moved past me.

"Dreek." He never said a word, which is worse than cursing me out.

"TAKE EM ALL OUT." Dreek said in his earpiece. He looked at me and walked away. I tried to run after him but shots rang out and it was a war zone.

# Jiao

"DREEK WAIT!" I yelled out and started running behind him.

"Get down Jiao." I heard someone yell but ignored them. Guns were going off left and right. At first, I wondered what the hell they were shooting at, but once Dreek told his guys to shoot, Hector's people showed up out of nowhere.

"DREEK PLEASE LISTEN TO ME." He never turned around.

I saw him jump in his car and pull off. I fell to my knees and cried my eyes out. I should've told him about Hector a long time ago, but what for? I didn't know who Dreek was at the time and the shit Mandy said is far from the truth. I know she only mentioned it, in hopes to get Dreek back in bed. *FUCK! I need to get my son.* I stood up when the gunfire ceased and it appeared to be quiet, besides some people cursing.

I pulled myself together and looked around, only to be hit by something. It started hurting but I didn't care, because once I saw Mandy's dumb ass getting in the car, I made it my business to get her. The closer I got, the more my blood boiled and my anger grew. The bitch had the nerve to smirk when she saw me coming.

I ran straight to her and did a high kick to her face. She fell into the car and that was all she wrote. My fists connected with her face so many times, I'm almost positive I broke her jaw. Someone tried to pull me off, but it didn't stop me from kicking her in the face and anywhere else before they could get me away.

"Calm down ma." My pressure was probably sky high and my breathing was erratic.

"Get the fuck off me." I broke free, went back to Mandy and stomped her ass out. Once again, my body was lifted off the ground and this time, thrown to the ground.

"That's enough Jiao."

"FUCK YOU BASTARD! WHY THE FUCK ARE YOU HERE?" I spit on him and walked towards my car.

"Don't fuck with me Jiao." I heard a gun click and stopped.

"We don't need guns right now, Ernesto." Hector said and put his hand over his, to drop the gun.

"Goodbye Hector."

"Go check on your son Jiao but you will meet me tomorrow or.-"

"Or what Hector? Huh? You're going to threaten to kill me, my son, or my father?" He came close to me.

"Tsk, Tsk, Tsk. Jiao, Jiao, Jiao. I would never kill you baby girl; especially when I still haven't felt in between those legs. But in due time, I'm going to handle this body, real, real well." He walked around me and squeezed my ass. I chuckled at his ignorance.

"Hector, you will never, ever in your pathetic life get another taste of this pussy." I dug my hand in my sweats, let some of my juices touch my fingers and pulled them out.

"You see, Dreek is the only man who will ever know what it feels and taste like. Mmmm, just thinking about how he handles my body, makes me want to go hop a ride on it." I put my fingers close to his lips to pretend I'd let him taste and pulled them back.

"Yea, my pussy taste real good too Hector." I teased and placed my fingers in my mouth. He licked his lips and grabbed me by the shirt.

"Don't play games with me Jiao. You know I always get what I want." He slid his tongue in my mouth and instead of pulling away, I wrapped my arms around his neck and continued with it. Sometimes a bitch has to do, what a bitch has to do. I felt his hand sliding down to my ass, then into my sweats. I pushed him off.

"Just like I remember. Go home and meet me here tomorrow." He handed me a piece of paper with an address on it, smacked me on the ass and turned around to leave.

"Get my stupid ass cousin up off the ground." He barked to his workers. I walked down to my car and noticed someone inside. I thought it was Sommer but nope, it wasn't.

"What are you doing here Jaime?"

"What am I doing? The question is, what are you doing and why are you bleeding?" When he said it, I remembered I was hit. My adrenaline must've been pumping so hard, I didn't even realize it. I wonder why Hector didn't say anything, but then again, it is dark as fuck out here.

"Fuck if I know." I lifted my shirt up and noticed blood leaking out of my side. Once I laid eyes on it, my vision became blurry and I was lightheaded.

"Get out the car Jiao." I heard him yelling but I couldn't move.

"Just go Jaime. I'll be fine." He opened the car door but sat there.

"Let me help you."

"I'm fine and why would you help me? You said I fucked up big time." I balled up a jacket I had in the back seat and pressed hard on the spot that was bleeding.

"Dreek told me to make sure you got home safe." I couldn't do shit but laugh.

"FUCK DREEK! FUCK HIM! FUCK HIM! FUCK HIM!" I started punching Jaime and pushing him out the car. My adrenaline started pumping again.

"Calm down Jiao."

"Calm down. You want me to calm down when my so-called man left me in a fucking war zone? Let's not even discuss how he had a got damn laser on my chest. He didn't even let me explain Jaime. He just left me. He left me." I found myself crying harder and once again my body became weaker.

"Jiao let me get you to a doctor."

"Fine. Come on the driver side and I'll move over." He agreed and the second he stepped out the car, I sped away. I could see him in the background shaking his head and dialing someone on his phone.

I dialed Sommer over and over and she wouldn't answer. After the last attempt, she shut her phone off. *Fuck it!* I drove until I found a hospital and parked in the front. I ran in and passed out on the ground.

****

"How are you today?" I opened my eyes and some short brown skin nurse had a smile on her face. She didn't look to be older than forty but now a days women aren't looking their age at all.

"I'm ok. Where am I?" I looked around. I noticed balloons and flowers but didn't bother to see who they were from. The only thing on my mind, is why I woke up here, alone?

"You are in Robert Wood Johnson hospital, here in New Brunswick."

"How long have I been here?" I asked as she checked my vitals.

"Three days." I hopped up out and started asking for my things.

"Miss Kim are you ok?" I snapped my neck and stared at her.

"How do you know my name?"

"Well the car you left running had your purse in it, as well as your identification." She passed me a clear plastic bag with my belongings inside.

"Oh."

"I was going to contact your family but before you went into surgery, the doctor told us you kept saying, not to call your family because they were dead. Is that true?" This

21

bitch is nosy as hell. I sat there thinking about Sommer who wouldn't answer her phone for me. My mom was gone, my father was on my shit list and the only person I had, is my son.

"Yes. I have no one but my son and he's a baby."

I pulled my phone out, powered it on and was about to show her pictures, when tons of text messages popped up. They were from Dreek's mom, Jaime, Hector, and my father. None from Dreek, which deep inside I wished they were. I'm sure Dreek had Jaime and his mom checking on me for him, but it's all good. The most shocking revelation, is Sommer hadn't contacted me either. I know she had no idea about Hector but it's not what Mandy made it seem, and as my friend, she should've been the main one here or texting. I started going through my messages as I waited for the nurse to finish taking my vitals.

**Hector:** *I don't see you here.*

**Hector:** *You think I'm playing.*

**Hector:** *I'm going to kill that Puta boyfriend of yours and maybe your son.*

I didn't even dwell on his stupid message about my son because one thing he doesn't do, is kill kids. He has four of his own and always told me how he couldn't imagine killing an innocent child, regardless of how fucked up their parents were. He'd make them an orphan instead.

**Ma:** *Where are you Jiao? I'm worried. You left and never came back.*

**Ma:** *What is going on? Dreek came here trying to take the kids so you wouldn't see them but I didn't let him. He won't tell me what happened. Call me.*

**Ma:** *Now I'm worried J. Where are you? It's not like you to leave your son or Dree. Please call or text so I know you're ok.*

Her messages went on and on, just like Jaime's and my fathers. Everyone wanted to know where I was all of a sudden. Fuck all of them. I'll take Dree and lil Dreek with me and bounce. She may not be my daughter but she's close enough and I'm sure he knows I would too, that's why he took his ass straight there.

"Can I leave today?"

23

"I don't see why not. Let me have the doctor come speak with you."

"Did they say where the blood came from?" She gave me a strange look.

"Honey, you were shot in the side. You lost a lot of blood and during surgery, you flat lined." Hearing I died, caused me to get scared. I didn't want to leave my kids, so I had to do better and in order to do that, I need to rid the toxins out of my life; starting with Hector.

I sent him a text and told him where I was. He wanted to come get me but I insisted on meeting him in a neutral spot. At this point, I gave zero fucks on who would see us. I lost Dreek because he listened to Mandy so there's nothing else to lose.

"Can you get my discharge papers so I can leave?" She nodded and left me. I picked the phone up and dialed Dreek's mom.

"Oh my God, Jiao. Where have you been? Are you ok?" She rambled so many questions off.

"I'm ok ma. I was shot and.-"

"SHOT! What the hell?" I started explaining what happened and heard someone start talk in the background of her house.

"I'm sorry for everything ma but I'm coming for my kids later."

"Ma, why do you keep holding him? He already spoiled as hell." I heard Dreek say. Even though we weren't speaking, I still got butterflies in my stomach listening to his voice.

"Please don't tell him its me."

"Dreek move. Don't you see me on the phone and have you found her yet?" I think she asked to get his response.

"No ma and right now it's what's best for both of us."

"Why? You won't tell me what happened."

"Some shit went down and right now I don't know what to believe."

"Dreek, you're letting your anger stop you from finding out the truth. Why do you keep doing her this way? She's going to leave you son and you won't be able to stop her."

"I'll see you later ma." I hung up because I didn't want to cry in her ear.

He doesn't trust me or know who I am and it hurts like hell, and for him to even think I'd go against him in anyway, is crazy. We've both confessed our feelings to each other, I had his son, showed him on more than one occasion I'm down for him and he still doesn't trust me. I think it's time to move on from this toxic relationship or whatever it is. After the nurse handed me my paperwork, I was on my way to start over.

# Hector

"Damn baby. You always look sexy." I stared at Jiao take a seat across from me and pick the menu up. Her beauty still captivated me and I had big plans for us, once I got rid of her baby daddy.

She called me three days after the shoot out and informed me of her whereabouts. We were supposed to meet up then, but something came up, so I had to reschedule. Here the two of us are, two weeks later sitting across from one another and a nigga couldn't stop staring.

"Let's get this over with. What are you here for? Why did you start shit with Dreek?"

"You really don't know do you?"

"Know what? How do you even know him?" She was confused as hell and it showed me that he kept her away from his business. Maybe he does love her, which is why it took me some time to find out about her. Everyone knew of Queenie and their fuck buddy status. From the outside looking in, it

27

may appear they were in love because he made it known she wasn't to be fucked with, but Queenie was no one.

However, as time went by, my informant, which I'm sure you all know is my cousin Mandy, let me know she was fucking Dreek. That was until Jiao locked him down by getting him to fall in love somehow. I can't even front because it shocked the hell out of me.

Dreek has never claimed a woman and over the last month or so, I kept hearing he fell hard for some chick. Unbeknownst to me, it's the same chick I fell for a few years back.

I know my cousin yelled out how Jiao set him up and played him this whole time but it's not true. Evidently, she had no idea about my beef with Dreek.

Jiao hated me for the way I treated her and it's the reason why we aren't together now, well that, and other reasons. I stared at her glancing down at the menu and a quick flashback of how we met and where we fell out.

*"Hey ma. You got a man?" I wasted no time asking questions.*

*See, I knew about a chick who did hits for the old Connect and I also knew he was retiring and had plans of passing the torch. Me, being in the drug game for so long, assumed he'd give it to me. Unfortunately, he handed it to those ignorant motherfuckers Dreek and Percy. Who had two people in power instead of one? I thought it was funny because we all know two people in charge never works out and one will kill the other. Needless to say, those two were thick as thieves and still are.*

*Anyway, the old Connect had her doing dangerous shit and she'd get away with it because of who she was, which is a female. Not to say females aren't killers but she by far, was deadly. I began watching her and even caught one death she did by accident and the shit was so gruesome, it made me want her on my team more.*

*Low and behold, I ended up doing some work with her father, who had people in China working for him or so I thought. Long story short, her pops owed me money and in return when he couldn't pay, he had to suffer the consequences and sadly, so did she.*

29

*When she arrived in China, I made it my business to take a trip there to meet her. It was hard to get her to agree for a sit down because she didn't know me. When we finally did, we met at a park, which I hate to be in public places in unknown areas, but I had to take the chance if I wanted her on my team. The two of us stayed at the park for hours talking and by the time we finished, I no longer wanted her to work for me but as my girl.*

*Weeks went on and she would take flights to Cuba and I would do the same to see her in China. I understood she was a virgin and not willing to lose her V card until she was ready. I gave her oral pleasure too many times to count and never expected anything from her. I respected her enough to wait. But like all men, when the cats away, the mice will play.*

*Therefore, I was having a party and she disappointed me and claimed she couldn't make it. I got over it and enjoyed the hell out of myself there. However, I took three bitches back to my place, which is the dumbest thing I could have ever done and we did all types of nasty shit.*

*The next morning, I woke up and all three bitches were dead with gunshots to their forehead and she sat in the chair with tears running down her face. I knew I fucked up because I promised and swore there were no other women and here she had three of them laid out. I tried pleading my case and even used the roofie line but she didn't fall for it. She told me she wanted to surprise me for my birthday and give me what we both wanted and it was for me to make love to her.*

*I stood up naked as the day I was born and it only infuriated her more. She even told me how she planned on killing me in my sleep too but then I would never see her move on and be happy without me. She never lied about that because Jiao has been on my mind since the moment she stepped out my life and I came back for her, but not for the reasons she thinks.* I admit it's going to be hard to reclaim her being she has a child now and clearly fell on love with the enemy but I'm going to change all that, starting now.

"Really Hector. How long are we going to sit here in silence?" She asked sipping out the straw.

31

"I'm admiring you is all. I miss you." She laughed. I was trying to get on her good side but she wasn't trying to hear it.

"Hector, I've told you over and over; we'll never be together again."

"You don't miss our long conversations and sitting up late watching the sunrise?" She smiled.

"I did but I found someone else to do those things with and much more. Hector, I don't know what's going on with you and Dreek but know this. I will have his back regardless of what he and I go through."

"You're going to have the back of a man who left you in a war zone to die? Huh?" I banged my fist on the table.

"His sons mother." I pointed to her.

"Had a fucking laser on her chest and if he said the word, you were gone."

"But he didn't." I shook my head laughing.

"He didn't have to Jiao. The fact it was even a possibility, should tell you something."

"And what's that?"

"He doesn't give a fuck about you Jiao. No matter what Mandy said, a real man wouldn't have turned his back on you in front of his enemy. You and I both know it." I could tell I was breaking her down by how watery her eyes were getting.

"Jiao, I know you love him but ask yourself this. Had I come for him, would you have left him standing there if a chick claimed he set you up?"

"No." She put her head down.

"Don't be embarrassed or ashamed because you did nothing wrong." I lifted her face up.

"Jiao, you've become weak for him and the Jiao I know, would have never allowed him to treat her this way." She wiped the tears that fell.

"Look Hector. Whatever you two have going on, please leave me and my kids out of it."

"Kids." I questioned.

"Yes kids. He has a daughter I've been raising and blood or not, she is mine." I nodded. I'm fully aware of the daughter.

"Jiao." We looked up at the woman and it was like she saw a ghost.

"Ma, what are you doing here?" She glanced at me and I gave her my million-dollar smile. Before I knew it, she tossed a cup of water on me. I hopped up out my seat and grabbed the bitch by her throat. She was trying to scratch, to get me to release her.

"Let her go." I heard a gun click and dropped the bitch on the ground. I knew it was Jiao and I knew she wouldn't shoot me here either. I kneeled down to make sure this lady heard me.

"You don't know me bitch and if I were you, I'd keep it that way or else your son will be burying you next to his father." I spit in her face and stood up.

Jiao had a weird look on her face.

"Let's go." I placed money on the table, snatched Jiao's hand and held it with a death grip. She started talking shit and I threw her in the back of my truck.

"Pull off."

"Let me out." She tried to punch me and I grabbed her by the hair.

"If you bite me, I will fucking kill you." She saw I wasn't playing and nodded.

I made her sit on my lap in a straddling position and kiss me. I knew she wanted to refuse but she had no choice. I unbuttoned her jeans and slid my hand inside.

"Cum for me like you used to Jiao."

"No Hector. Get offffffff. Oh shit. Oh shit." She threw her head back and started grinding on my fingers. I lifted her shirt with my other hand and pulled her bra over her titties. She may have been a virgin all those years ago but I still knew how to please her.

"Fuck this. Take those jeans off." I could see her getting nervous.

"Jiao, I would never hurt you." She nodded and removed her jeans and panties.

"Oh fuckkkkkkk." She moaned out when my mouth touched her pussy. She tried to fight the urge to cum and lost.

"Mmmmmm, you definitely taste as good as I remember." So much for me never tasting her again.

"Let me feel you." I said and sat her down on me before she could protest. Her pussy was extremely tight and a nigga was getting ready to cum.

"Oh my God Dreek. Yesssss." My dick got soft and I punched her so hard, she flew off my lap.

I lifted her up, banged her head against the window and told my driver to pull over. Before the truck came to a complete stop, I opened the door and tossed her out; naked and all. I didn't care if cars were behind us. She violated the fuck out of me by calling me his name. If she wanted to play games, then bitch it's on.

# Dreek

"How is she?" I asked my mom when she told me what happened to Jiao. She called me the minute Hector snatched Jiao out the restaurant and tossed her in his truck. I learned a lot from Jiao and if she didn't put up a fight, it's because she had a plan of her own. I hated she didn't listen but I also knew, she could hold her own until I got to her.

"I don't know yet. She's still in the back." I'm not sure what happened in the truck but my mom mentioned how she jumped in her own car and followed behind Hector's truck. After about ten minutes, he threw J out with no clothes on. Of course, I wanted his head on a platter now, but he seemed to disappear after. My mom stopped her car and tended to Jiao and I didn't blame her.

"Dreek, I'm ready." Sabrina said when she came in the room naked. My dick jumped at the sight.

"Andreek, I'm only going to say this once because you're grown and going to do what you want." I blew my breath because I knew what she was about to say.

"Jiao loves you and what you're about to indulge in, is eventually going to come out. All I'm going to say is, think about how you would feel if Jiao were in the same position as you with a man. How would you feel?" She hung up.

I laid back on the bed and seconds later felt Sabrina's hands sliding up my legs and then undoing my jeans. I feel bad but right now I need to relieve this stress and Jiao and I are not even on speaking terms.

"Shit Sabrina." She was doing the damn thing with her mouth but all I could do is envision Jiao doing it.

"Fuck me Dreek." She tried sitting on my dick without a condom.

I moved her off and pulled one out my pocket. Sabrina been on some other shit lately and after today, I plan on cutting her off permanently. Granted, I did when Jiao became my girl but once all the shit went down, I flew out here to Cuba to handle business and as usual, Sabrina greeted me.

"Yes Dreek. Yes baby. Oh fuck." She grabbed the pillow to cover her mouth and let me beat the pussy up. When we finished, she flat out told me her pussy was swollen and she couldn't walk. I laughed and told her to take her ass to sleep if it's that bad.

I jumped in the shower, put some basketball shorts on with a wife beater and made my way into the living room of the suite. I sat on the couch, flipped the television on and picked my phone up. I had a few missed calls from my mom, one from Jaime and another from Percy. I hit my mom up because she was most likely calling with an update on J.

"Boy, where you been?"

"What's up ma?" I ignored her question and took a pull of the blunt I just lit.

"Jiao woke up, left the hospital and no one can find her."

"What you mean no one can find her?" I stood up and started pacing the room.

"Just what I said. I've been waiting in this emergency department for hours and no one ever came out. I went to the nurses' station and the look she gave me let me know something wasn't right. The doctor came out and told me she was discharged two hours previously."

"Did he say if she was ok?"

"She had some cracked ribs, a concussion and a gash, he had to stitch up on the side of her face but otherwise she's good. He tried to tell her to stay but she refused and told him if he didn't sign the papers, she'd have him murdered." I had to laugh.

"Dreek, I don't give a fuck what you doing with some other bitch. Get your ass back here and find her."

"I'll be there in a few days." My mom tried to curse me out more but I hung up and called Jaime.

"Home girl done went rogue bro." He said when he answered.

"What you mean she went rogue?"

"Just what I said. She bounced from the hospital and went to your spot. She fucked your cars up worse than before. Broke all the windows out your house and I can't tell you what she did to the inside but she was in there for some time." I sat down grinning. Jiao was letting me know I fucked up in her own way.

"Man, she went to Queenie's house and when she answered the door, J drop kicked and beat the shit out of her."

"Yo, don't tell me you watched." I took another pull from the blunt.

"You asked me to keep an eye on her from a distance, so that's what I did."

"Anyway, let me finish telling you." I shook my head listening to him tell me how she went to Mandy's house, set the shit on fire and watched it burn.

"Where is she now?"

"Putting luggage in her truck." I almost choked when he said that.

"Where the fuck she going?"

"It looks like away from here."

"She better not take my kids." I don't know why I said that when she's their mother.

"Too late. Dree is getting in the passenger side and she has lil man in his car seat."

"It's fine. They missed her." I blew my breath and rested my head on the couch.

"I'll be here for another day. Keep an eye on her and I'll see her when I get back." He agreed and hung up. I returned Percy's call next.

"How is she Dreek?" Sommer asked. I guess she is the one who called.

"I haven't spoken to her Sommer but you dead ass wrong."

"How am I wrong?"

"Because she's your best friend and I know for a fact she's reached out to you a bunch of times and you refused all her calls."

"Dreek, I didn't know she had done those things. Percy is my son's father and to know she plotted on him too, broke what friendship I thought we had."

"Sommer, on some real shit. I love the fuck out of Jiao and I'm going to hear her out, just not right now. However, you are her best friend, her sister and she needed you. I can see if she plotted on you. You left her hanging, yet, you calling me for updates."

"Dreek, how can you even?-"

"Because the plot was supposedly on me, so I have every right to be mad. Man, put Percy on." I wasn't about to go back and forth with her. She could beat me in the head all day about how wrong Jiao was but she's supposed to listen to the truth before ignoring her. I am too, but everyone knows how I get down.

"What up?" Percy asked in the phone.

"Nothing. You called."

43

"Oh yea. Jaime told me what your girl did."

Both of us started laughing.

"How's it going over there?" He asked referring to me getting shit popping.

"We go in tomorrow."

"You sure you don't need me to come?"

"Nah. You still making up with your girl, I'm good. Valdez, is meeting up in the morning. I'll keep you updated." After we spoke for a few more minutes, I laid on the couch and fell asleep. I woke up to Sabrina giving me head again and more sex.

"I'm out yo."

"When's the next time you coming back?" She asked and I really didn't have time to talk. I sat her down her down anyway and told her what it was.

"Sabrina, I'm with someone and.-"

"Oh, the Chinese bitch." I smacked the shit out of her.

"Don't call her that and how do you even know about her?" She wiped her mouth and stared at me.

"Millie told me." Millie is the chick Percy messed with a few times but cut her off when she pretended she was in love.

"Like I was saying, she's my girl and what you and I have is over."

"Dreek, why can't it stay the way it was? She won't know." It's like watching Queenie all over. The begging started and so did the offering of sex again. I pushed her off and bounced. I didn't need any bullshit right now with what I'm about to do.

Valdez met me downstairs and we drove to the spot we were about to hit. He informed me of all the security in place, as well as the workers. I knew what time they came in, switched shifts and any other important information needed. We went to the spot and stayed there until the sun went down. The crazy part is Hector is supposed to be this big time, wanna be connect, however, not once did anyone approach our vehicle to ask why we were sitting here. Amateur shit at its best.

At midnight, I hit the person up who's making this possible and told him its time. Valdez and I stepped out the car and watched as four helicopters came and circled the fields Hector had growing his product in. I typed in the word *Ready* and four bombs dropped in the fields making them burn immediately. The fire ripped up and down the fields like a raging wildfire. Security came out and began running around like chickens with their heads cut off.

"Next stop. Hector's condo." Throughout the night we hit most of Hector's hideout spots, a few of his warehouses and some brothel shit he ran. Motherfuckers were scrambling like crazy. Once we were done, I shook hands with Valdez and had him take me to the airport.

"Job well done."

"See you soon." Valdez gave me a pound and I walked through the airport with a grin on my face.

Most people would think I'd be nervous about him retaliating. Nah, he's not smart enough because if he were, he'd be ready for the unexpected and he wasn't. It's all good though. His time is coming and when it does, I'm going to make sure he suffers for putting hands on my mom and my girl.

# Mandy

"Hector, you have to kill her." I told him in a light whisper. Don't ask me why I'm whispering when no one is here.

It's been a couple of weeks since the shit went down with Jiao. The bitch almost broke my jaw and burned my house down to the ground. From what my neighbor says, she stood there watching it. I knew it was her because there's no one out here crazy enough to do no shit like that, except her and Dreek. Now, I've been shacked up in a crappy motel waiting for my cousin to hook me up with an apartment but he's procrastinating.

"I'm not discussing her with you. What I need you to do is try and find out where Dreek is. He came over here and did some shit and he needs to be dealt with." I saw him the other day, so he's clearly not in hiding. I thought to myself but wouldn't dare say it out loud.

48

Secretly, I think my cousin wanted to be Dreek but he didn't have the balls to pull off half the shit Mr. Puryear did. Yea, Hector may be feared over in Cuba but Dreek is feared everywhere and that type of power, is what any man would want.

"Hector, Dreek has been around and you must be crazy if you think, I'm going anywhere near him after what I did."

Yes, I am the one who shot him outside the bathroom. He made me so mad when he embarrassed me that I ran outside and came back in without being re checked by security. I told him I had to get a tampon out my car and he believed me. Anyway, I caught Dreek coming out. He paid me no mind and pushed me away. The first shot scared me and he smiled.

I've never shot a gun before and I felt like everyone heard it but with the music blasted, no one did. He threatened me and I let off two more times and promised to kill Jiao next. I ran out the club like a prisoner escaping a jail.

49

The same night Hector popped up and we went to find Dreek to kill him. I hadn't told him what I did. The only reason I wasn't scared outside the warehouse, is because my cousin was there with his men and Dreek was more interested in finding out how Jiao and Hector knew one another.

It was pretty funny how he walked away from her as she screamed out his name but I knew, like everyone else, he'd be back for her. Maybe not right now, but love was written all over his face. That shit doesn't go away in a day, night or even a week. I do know I'm going to get her back and this time, she or no one else will see it coming. I'm getting pretty tired of her beatings and it's time to show and prove.

"Do what I said Mandy or I'll make sure you won't see the light of day." I sucked my teeth and hung up. How the hell is he going to threaten me because he can't find Dreek? That's the bullshit I be talking about.

\*\*\*\*

50

"Hey Mandy." Queenie said and opened the door. No, we weren't best friends but we had the same agenda when it came to Jiao.

"Can I come in?" She stepped aside for me to walk in and surprisingly Marcus was in the living room with the baby on his chest. I looked at her and she shrugged her shoulders. She was playing with fire and its best I say what I need to and get the fuck out of here and fast.

"Let's talk in the kitchen." I followed her and sat at the table.

"Are you crazy having him in here?" I shouted but more or less in a whisper.

"Why is that? She's his daughter?"

"How do you know? The last time we spoke, you weren't even sleeping with him." She sucked her teeth.

"Anyway, Dreek came in the hospital when I delivered and beat the shit out of Marcus for holding him."

"Get the fuck out of here."

"Swear to God. Mind you, Marcus was holding her and had I not jumped up and caught her, my baby would've been on the ground probably with a crushed skull. I know Dreek is crazy but he didn't even care Marcus had her in his hands."

"Queenie, I'm not taking his side but he had a right to be mad." She rolled her eyes.

"You had him believing the baby was his and then he comes to see, and you have another nigga holding his so-called child before him. What did you expect?"

"He could've at least let me grab the baby and gave Marcus a fair fight."

"Queenie listen to yourself. You're trying to make it right for what you did." I don't even know why I said anything because she starting going on and on about how Marcus could have beaten Dreek up. I wanted to laugh but she was dead serious.

"Listen, fuck all that. We need to get Jiao and fast."

"I'm over the bitch and honestly, Marcus and I are moving away this weekend."

"WHAT?" I yelled and scared her.

"I'm not sitting around waiting for Dreek to come take a test, if he still wants one and find out she isn't his. Once we're far away, I'll send him a letter and the test results and he'll see for himself. I gave Dreek some of the best years of my life and then he comes over here talking about he put me before his daughter and should have left me alone a long time ago. And don't get me started on how the Chinese bitch came over a week ago, and soon as I opened the door, she kicked me in the face and we sat out here fighting. To be honest, now that I have my daughter, I'm over all this petty shit. I sat back and reevaluated my life and realized I never should have stayed with him this long."

"I get it but don't you want to get her back since you can't get him."

"Didn't you just hear me say I'm over it?"

"Yea, but come on Queenie. Let's get her ass once for the road." I noticed her thinking about it.

"YO, GET THE FUCK OUT OF HERE!" I heard behind me.

"What?"

"You heard me. She said the bullshit is over and you're sitting here trying to pressure her into the shit. If you want to get the chick back do it on your own because she isn't participating."

"I see you found another controlling nigga."

"What bitch." He came closer and if we were anywhere else, I'd probably fuck him. His cologne, swag and the demeanor turned me on for some reason. I wonder if it's how he got Queenie? I mean shit, he did work for Dreek and yet, still fucked with her.

"Yo, get your friend Queenie. Her nasty ass wanna fuck." I smirked and pushed past him.

"Mandy, I gave you a pass with Dreek because we all knew he was for everyone, but this one right here." She pointed to Marcus.

"Is off limits. I promise you if you even think about kissing his cheek, I'll whoop your ass worse than the Chinese chick." She slammed the door in my face. Oh, this bitch wanna talk shit. I got something for that ass. I picked my phone up and started texting.

**Me:** *Hey Dreek. I know you don't want to hear from me, but I thought you'd like to know, Queenie has one of your workers named Marcus at her house and he had your daughter asleep on his chest.* Send! Now let's see who gets the last fucking laugh now.

# Queenie

"Get your shit." Marcus yelled and started snatching up our daughters' things. Like I told Mandy, this is his daughter.

After Dreek's crazy ass left the hospital, I called a nurse in and she called for a doctor to come. They took Marcus out the room and had him checked out down in the emergency room. When he came back up, I decided to have him tested for his own reasons. I knew for a fact she was his, but he wanted the results in case Dreek ever tried to take her. I understood and didn't mind.

The day Dreek told me it was over, I went to him and we've been together every day since then. We spent as much time as we could without getting caught. I never complained when he didn't come in until the wee hours of the morning because I knew he was making as much money as he possibly could, so we can leave.

He doesn't have money like Dreek. But I'm willing to compromise to be happy and he does that for me. Sometimes the price of living the glamorous life isn't worth the bullshit and Marcus made me see that. I will always love Dreek and have a soft spot for him but our time has come to an end.

"Why are we leaving?" I asked when he came back in the house and grabbed the baby.

"Because she just either called or text him."

"I doubt it."

"Stop being gullible Queenie. I'm telling you she sneaky and once you snapped on her, it's exactly what she did." I grabbed my purse, phone, keys and any other small things I could. He told me to leave the rest and to get in the car.

"What's in the bag?" I tossed the big duffle bag in the trunk.

"I may be gullible, naïve, and ignorant but a bitch has never been stupid. That's about two hundred thousand dollars. Dreek gave me thousands on a daily basis and I started saving when he showed me signs of feeling the Chinese chick."

"That's my girl." He leaned in to kiss me and the glass to one of the side windows shattered.

"GET DOWN!" He yelled and zoomed out the parking lot. I guess he wasn't lying about Mandy telling him.

"Shit, these niggas are on my ass." I looked in the rearview mirror and it was a black truck following us.

"Oh shit. It's the Chinese bitch."

"What?"

"I know her truck. It's a Cayenne and I'm pretty sure Dreek got it for her." As I said it, she bumped the back of his car.

"Oh shit. I ain't running from no bitch." It was dark outside and no traffic. Why in the hell did he drive down a street like this?

He stopped short and she swerved on the side. She hit the side of the car and it pushed us onto a curb.

I looked over and she had her truck facing us with the lights on and she was revving her engine. I got scared because it was on the side my daughter was on. I opened the door and put my hands up. She drove her car to me, stopped in front of me with the bumper barely missing my body and jumped out.

"What the fuck Jiao?" Marcus said and she looked over to see him.

"Marcus, I didn't know it was you driving. Fool, you should've pulled over sooner." My daughter started crying.

"Tell me that's not your kid."

"Yea, she mine." He went to the back to get her out the seat. She walked over to him and stared at my baby.

"Too bad you'll never know your mother."

*POW!* I heard and fell to the ground. My leg was in excruciating pain. She came over and punched me a few times in the face. I tried to fight back but it was no way I could with a gunshot wound in my leg.

"I can't beat your ass enough for treating my daughter wrong for all those years." She kicked me in the stomach and I damn near vomited.

"What do you want Jiao? I'm leaving with him and I promise to never both you again. Please let me go." She started laughing and looked at Marcus, who was shaking his head.

"Queenie, you have been nothing but a pain in my ass since I came on the scene. Most people would have left well enough alone but you, you continued with the bullshit and I'm not sure if anyone told you, but I'm not the bitch you ever want on your bad side."

"Marcus, I need help. Why are you standing there? Kill her or something."

"Let me tell you a few things before you die, because it looks like you're losing a lot of blood, so you won't be here too much longer." I gave her a crazy look.

"When I found out about Marcus the day I beat your ass at the store, I went and told him I was going to kill you. At first, he begged me not to because of your daughter and how he was indeed in love with you. However, once I told him you drugged my man and had slept with him with his child in your stomach, he was disgusted." I felt tears coming down my face.

"He really did love you Queenie but you were selfish and wanted nothing more than to hurt me, by continuing to sleep with Dreek, who by the way, knows nothing about this." She pointed to all of us.

"Anyway, he was hurt because he thought you loved him enough to leave Dreek and be with only him."

"I am in love with you Marcus."

"The funny thing about that is, I had Dreek's phone one day and sent the messages you were sending him. He knows how you wanted to suck Dreek off and even offered him to do threesomes, just to keep him around. You knew he and I were exclusive so I sent them to Marcus to inform him, that killing you is the best thing."

"Marcus, please think about our daughter."

61

"You did this Queenie. Why couldn't you just be with me?"

"Marcus, you know why."

"No, I know what you told me. We could have left a long time ago."

"Listen." She looked at me.

"You're going to die, for sure." She gave me a fake smile.

"I'm going to give you one minute to say goodbye to your daughter. If you take longer than sixty seconds, I promise to splatter your brains while you have her in your arms." I underestimated the shit out of this bitch.

"Jiao."

"Marcus hand her the baby so I can get this shit over with. I have a few more appearances to make." He handed her the baby and asked me not to miss if she took too long. I squeezed my daughter and cried my eyes out. I was hysterical and couldn't even get the words out to say I love you to her.

"50, 51, 52, 53,"

"Wait Jiao. Let me get my daughter first." She held the gun in my face and watched Marcus take my baby.

"Was Dreek worth all this?" Were the last words I heard before everything went black.

# Jiao

"Thanks J. I don't think I could do it." Marcus said and gave me a hug.

"I don't have beef with you but Dreek won't excuse the shit. You need to leave town now and never return." He walked to the car, strapped his daughter in and pulled off.

Marcus is a cool cat from the little I know about him. Unfortunately, he got caught up with dumb ass Queenie and now his daughter will grow up without a mom. The crazy part is, he really loved her and she played with his heart, which is why he had no problem with me offing her. Not that I cared because she was dying regardless. It made it easier that he didn't fight me though.

After I left Queenie, I hit Jaime up and told him they needed a cleaning lady on the street I left her at. He laughed and told me to stop running around rampant and sit my ass down. Shit, at this point, my ass could care less about going to jail. These motherfuckers were testing my gangsta.

I'm far from a savage but I do get down and dirty when needed, which is why Hector and I even linked up in the first place. He wanted me on his team, however, after talking to him and his hearing how sheisty he was, I couldn't be a part of it. I did end up falling for him, he hurt me, I left and now he came back.

Hector is a guy who throws a tantrum if he doesn't get his way. For example, take what he did to me in the restaurant. He wanted me to say I wouldn't ever fuck with Dreek again for leaving me to die and I may not, but its none of his business. My relationship with my kids' father is way deeper than anything Hector and I shared. The two didn't even compare. Then he tried to choke Dreek's mom and I pulled my gun on him. I wanted to kill him right there but there's a time and place for everything.

I enjoyed the way he ate my pussy in the truck but its only because I imagined it being Dreek. When

65

he sat me on top of him, I was being reckless because we had no protection but there's a method to my madness. I knew he'd get upset by me moaning Dreek's name. I didn't think he'd toss me out the truck but I survived.

The tracking device was placed inside during the time he tried to fuck, and at this very moment, I could tell where those trucks were. Shockingly, they haven't moved in a few days. I figured he went to Cuba but when he returns, when those trucks move so will I. I could go to Cuba but I'm sure everyone over there knows by now about me and he has them on alert.

The day we were at Mandy's house and I smelled his cologne, I became terrified because it meant he found me. He wanted me dead for leaving him and always told me if he couldn't have me, then no one else would. Hector may be portraying himself as a man who wants me but it's all an act.

He used to send me tons of threatening messages about knowing what I did to Bash. In the beginning, I wondered how he knew but it all came to me when he put in one of his texts, that he had eyes everywhere. He claimed to have found out about Dreek's brother being shot and since I did hits and left suddenly, he put two and two together. I still call bullshit but until I find out how he really knows, I'll keep quiet.

Anyway, the night of the shooting at the club; I watched the guys come in and point their guns straight at me. I knew Hector sent them because they were from out of town and he had been working endlessly to find me. Sommer told me, Percy told her they assumed it was guys trying to take their spots but I knew different and left it alone.

I never contacted Hector and let him know, I knew and kept going on with my life. Hector may be a bitch about certain situations but he's as deadly as Dreek and if he says I won't be with anyone but him, I believe it. He's going to come for me and I plan on being ready.

67

****

"Hello daddy." I opened the door to his house and found him at the kitchen table looking nervous as hell. I haven't been here since I found the money and diaries my mom left.

"Jiao. Oh my God. You're ok. I've been calling you for days." He checked me over and gave me a hug. Something was suspect as hell and I knew it had everything to do with the envelope I found it the house a while back. The letter read, *give me what you owe me or I'm taking it.*

"How much did you owe him and what did you promise?"

"What?" He let go and stared at me. I pulled the letter out my pocket and threw it on the table.

"When did you get this?"

"The day I came to get mommy's things."

"Jiao, I.-"

"Tell her." I saw a gun pointed at my father's head and came face to face with Bash.

"Bash, what the fuck is going on? Why are you here?"

"Sit down Jiao."

"Hell no. What the fuck?"

"DO I LOOK LIKE I'M FUCKING ASKING YOU TO SIT. DON'T MAKE ME SAY IT AGAIN." I've never seen the look Bash had in his eyes; not even when I shot him. I was scared for my father and knew whatever Bash wanted him to tell me was about to hurt me and take him away. I sat in the seat.

"TELL HER NOW!" Bash yelled out and my father began to speak.

"Jiao, a long time ago I got involved with a guy who I went to for drugs."

"Drugs! What are you talking about?"

"You know Sommer's dad and I are friends and he used to be heavy in the drug game." I nodded.

"Ok."

"Well, I wanted to get in on making more money but he wouldn't let me. He offered me what I

69

needed but I refused to take a handout and wanted to work for it." I looked at my father like he was crazy. What Chinese man sold drugs? The shit doesn't even sound right.

"I ended up hearing about another guy who could front me the drugs and I would pay later and that was Hector. He and I made a deal that as long as I paid him a certain amount monthly, it was fine.

In the beginning, everything went smooth but on some occasions, I had to put our own money in to make sure he got paid. Long story short, people in China don't get high like over here. Either that or I trusted the wrong people over there."

"Ok. What does Bash have to do with this?" I looked at Bash and he was itching to pull the trigger, which made me want my dad to speak faster so I know what happened.

"When I couldn't pay he came here and.-" He put his head down.

"TELL HER." Bash hit him in the head with the gun and blood squirted out his eye.

70

"BASH STOP!"

"SIT THE FUCK DOWN JIAO AND DON'T MAKE ME SAY IT AGAIN." This time he pushed me to the chair.

"I'm sorry Jiao. I didn't mean to. You know I loved your mother." It was like the air left my body and I could no longer breathe.

"He was going to kill you or her and I had to make a decision." I covered my mouth and felt the tears falling down my face.

"Hector told me your mother was the better choice because she was having an affair and at first, I told him he was lying. He started sending me photos of this man here and your mom out on dates and on vacations."

"What did you expect dad? You were cheating and beating on her." He put his head down.

"What else happened? Please don't tell me you killed her."

"I could never kill her."

"Somebody did."

71

"The day she went to the hotel to meet him, Hector had some guys snatch me up and they followed her. They asked the receptionist what her room number was and we went to her floor. Your mom opened the door in just some heels and a lingerie set and it enraged me to see her about to make love to someone else. I called her a whore and hit her a few times." He stopped talking. I noticed Bash wipe his eye.

"Keep going."

"She yelled out how hurt you would be and that she thought I loved her. She reached out for me and I wanted to grab her and say it would be ok but a bullet entered a stomach. I turned around and Hector was standing there holding a gun and shot her again. He called her a whore too and they dragged me out and told me to stay home and not mention shit. If I ever told, you were next. I'm sorry Jiao." I jumped over the table and started fighting my father. I took every frustration out on him. Bash allowed me to fight him until I got tired. My dad didn't even attempt to stop me.

"I got this J. Do you want me to call my brother to come get you?" I shook my head no.

"You sure about this?" I nodded.

"How could you?"

"I'm sorry J but I need to tell you this."

"I don't want to hear shit you have to say." I got up to leave.

"Hector didn't meet you in China by accident or to get you to work for him."

"What are you talking about? I never worked for him."

"Exactly! His plan was to pretend he needed you on his team, get you to fall for him and then he'd kill you. When you left him alone, he became even more relentless to get you. I don't know why it took him so long, but there's always a reason for the things he does."

"What?"

"Jiao, I still owe him and wants his money."

"That's not my problem."

"I know you can take care of yourself and I'm sure his brother." He pointed to Bash.

"Won't allow anyone to hurt you but be careful. He tried to take the businesses, which is why I made sure to put them in your name. Get away Jiao. I love you." I wiped my

eyes and nodded at Bash.

*PHEW! PHEW!*

He shot my father twice and I watched his body slump

over. I saw both of my parents take their last breath but the

only one that hurts, is my mom. Now that I know everything,

I'm going to make sure Hector pays for it.

# Bash

"You good." Dreek asked on the phone when I called to tell him I needed a clean-up. Jiao asked me not to contact him until she left but he knew where I was, and waiting to hear from me.

"Yea. I'm glad I know what really happened to her."

"Does J know?"

"She came when I was about to kill him. I made him tell her."

"WHAT?" He yelled in the phone.

"Dreek, I know you wanted to be here to support her but I couldn't wait on you to get rid of the attitude. The way you treated and left her that night is fucked up and if no one else will tell you, I will. Jiao has suffered a lot bro and you were her support system. The one who promised not to leave or hurt her and you did both. The most fucked up part about it, is that you did it in front of your enemy. I can tell you he's probably in her ear saying you aren't the right man for her.

Who leaves their kids mother in a war zone?" He sat on the phone in silence. I checked to make sure he didn't hang up.

"Look, I have to make some moves. I'll talk to you in a few."

"Where is she?" I stared at her as she stood in the door waiting for me. She mentioned going to her mom's grave and I wanted to go too.

"She left after I killed him." If Jiao wanted to talk, then she'll get in touch with him. I heard the beeping noise and noticed he hung up.

"Thanks for not telling him."

"Jiao look. I know you still love him and vice versa but know that even though he left you that night, you were never in harm's way. He made sure of it." She turned to look at me.

"How could you say that?"

"He needs to be the one to tell you and he will." I left it alone and followed her in my car to the cemetery.

Once we got there, I let her go first. She was worried Dreek would show up, which he most likely would. He told me before, she visited her a lot and now that her dad is gone, he'd probably put it together. After she stood up, she walked over to another grave and cleaned it off. Instead of speaking to her mom, I followed and noticed it was Dree's mom.

"Dree would have a fit if she saw all these leaves on her mom's grave." She cleaned it off.

"Thanks for being a good role model for my niece. Out of all the women my brother may have been with, you are the only one who has had such an impact on his and her life. I was gone for three years but he and I spoke everyday. He told me about the beef with Dree and Queenie. I know some may judge him for keeping her around but he really wanted a woman to help him raise her. Shit, he doesn't know a thing about raising a girl. Before you say it, yes my mom is there but it's different."

"I know and regardless of what we go through, I'd never neglect her. That's my daughter and I'm going to raise her the best I can." She said and glanced down at Dree's mom grave.

"Her mom would be so proud right now to see how she's maturing."

77

"She knows and so does my brother. Trust me, he learned his lesson keeping Queenie around. I don't think he'd allow another woman around Dree anyway. Shit, I don't think Dree would allow it either. I saw what you did to Mandy." We both started laughing.

"I miss him so much Bash."

"I know and he feels the same." She wiped her eyes.

"He's confused right now J. Put yourself in his shoes. You wouldn't know what to believe either. Give him time."

"I'm trying to understand but he left me Bash."

"Again, he left you standing there but you weren't alone and haven't been."

"I was shot in the side Bash. How can you say that?"

"And the person was killed at the same time." She looked confused.

"Jiao, let him explain it to you."

"Its ok. No matter what he says right now, I'm not going to believe him. He's already sleeping with some bitch in Cuba, so I'm done."

"Who told you that?"

"Hector had a lot to say." She rolled her eyes.

"Remember, he's making sure I never fuck with your brother again and right now, he's doing everything to make me not want to. Do me a favor Bash?" She started walking away.

"Tell your brother, the love I thought we shared, should've brought him home to me and not into the arms of another woman." She opened her car door, sat down and pulled off.

I walked over to her mom's grave and sat there for two hours speaking about everything. People say you feel a presence sometimes when you visit a loved one and I used to think it was a lie.

I swear Candiance was sitting next to me with her head on my shoulder. It sounds crazy and I know it's not possible but it didn't hurt to have those feelings. When I got in my car to leave, I glanced at her grave and a ton of butterflies sat on top of the tombstone. I smiled because she adored those things. I drove off smiling; today was surely a good day for me.

****

I rang the doorbell to Cameron's house and Jaime came to the door barely dressed. I walked past him, went in the living room and saw Dree and her brother. I asked what they were doing there and he told me Cameron asked Jiao to bring them over to meet their cousin.

Now my ass is confused like a motherfucker because we all knew who Jaime was. He shrugged his shoulders and told me Cameron was upstairs in the shower. I went up, locked the bedroom door and stripped down to join her.

"Mmmmm. I missed you baby." She turned around and wrapped her legs around my waist.

"I see." She moved up a little and slid down.

"Ssssss. Bash, I'm pregnant. Oh shit baby." She moaned out and I stopped.

"Are you fucking with me?" She smiled and shook her head no.

"Damn, I love you." I attacked her mouth with mine and stepped out the shower to make love to her. Shower sex is good but after the news she gave me, I wanted to show my appreciation. Dree knocked on the door a few times and I heard Jaime yelling at her.

"You ok Bash?" She asked. I had my arm covering my eyes.

"Hell yea. I'm happy as hell you're going to have my baby." She got on top of me.

"I'm seven weeks and the first doctor's appointment is next week."

"Wait. How did you know how far you were if you didn't go to the doctors yet?"

"Babe, I work on the baby floor."

"I forgot. What about your job? You're not going to get fired, are you?"

"No silly. I have maternity leave and.-"
"Take that shit now. I don't want anything happening to my baby."

"Bash, I'm fine. I promise to take my leave at six months but just so you know, I'm going to expect to be pampered."

"You already know."

"I love you Bash." She kissed me and got up.

"Where you going?"

"To play with the kids. I had Jiao drop them off and Jaime has had them because their uncle came in horny."

"Shit, that pussy is lethal and I'm in it every chance I get."

"Yo, I don't want to hear that shit." Cameron had opened the door. We didn't know Jaime was standing there.

"Nigga bye." Cameron walked over to me.

"That dick is lethal too and I'm killing a bitch if she tries to come for it." She stuck her tongue in my mouth.

"Alright yo, go get the kids Cameron damn. You know he ain't going nowhere." She stopped and smacked him on the way out the door.

"Yo. We need to get Dreek and J back together. The nigga getting on my nerves." I busted out laughing. Ever since my brother got with Jiao, everyone said she calmed him down but when they were broken up, he'd be on a rampage, which is exactly how he's been acting. I guess it's time to get them in the same room.

# Sommer

"Do you think I'm wrong for not speaking to Jiao?" I asked Percy. He was waiting to take me out to eat. I wanted to stay in but he refused and forced me to get dressed. I haven't been really leaving the house since finding out the shit with Jiao and this Hector dude.

"I told you don't ask me shit about Jiao. If you want to know how I would handle it, I wouldn't fuck with you anymore." He shrugged and left the room. Why didn't anyone understand where I was coming from?

"Percy."

"Let's go Sommer." He yelled from downstairs and I sat on the bed. All I had to do was grab my phone but the way he spoke, pissed me off and now I didn't want to go.

"I'm not about to fight with you." He lifted me over his shoulder, carried me down the steps and didn't put me down until we were in front of the car. I stared at him the entire ride to the restaurant. Percy was sexy as hell and all mine.

The restaurant had a grand opening sign on it and there were quite a few people in line. He walked past and inside. I looked around and it was big and had a laid-back atmosphere. Some restaurants are loud and have limited space but not this one.

"Miller for two." He told the hostess. She escorted us to a table in the back with little light. It was quite a bit of people in here too.

"This is nice baby."

"It is right. They play jazz here too."

"Really." He pointed to a band setting up.

"Hi, my name is Marissa. Can I take your drink order?" The waitress seemed nice. I almost snapped because she stared at Percy the entire time; even when taking my order.

"Come here baby." He slid closer to me. We were in a circular type of booth.

"No woman has my attention the way you do."

"Percy, she disrespectful as hell."

"Most women are but you're my queen so don't step off your throne to address peasants. Its beneath you and so is fighting." I nodded.

"Are you ready to order your food?"

"Yes, but can you send your manager over?"

"Is something wrong?"

"Not at all." She walked away and another chick came over. She was pretty too but she was respectful.

"Hey Mr. Miller. How are you?" He stood up and gave her a hug.

"Carol this is my fiancé Sommer. Sommer this is Carol, your general manager."

"Excuse me."

"Wow! She is gorgeous boss. I mean other boss."

"What is going on?"

"Babe, I brought you here tonight, to tell you, I brought this restaurant for you."

"WHAT?" I yelled and people stared at me.

"Miss, your name is on the door. The place is called Sommer's Finest Cuisine." I covered my mouth and started crying. I never paid attention to the name of the place coming in.

"I know how much you love to cook and thought you could bring your banging ass recipes here."

"Percy, this is too much."

"Nothing is ever too much for you. Let me show you around." He helped me up.

"Oh Carol, Marissa is fired." Percy told her.

"I'm on it."

"Percy no. What if she has kids or something?"

"It's your call Sommer. This is your spot and I'll be damned if anyone disrespects you." I thought about what he said and asked to speak to the woman.

"I'll have her meet you in your office."

"Percy, I already have a job and.-" He opened the door and my mouth dropped. The office was huge with top of the line furniture, technology devices and my degrees on the wall.

"Baby." I turned around and he pulled me in for a kiss.

"I can't wait to get you home."

"Why wait?" I asked and closed the door. I locked it and lifted my dress over my head.

"Damn babe. Your body is the shit." He ran his finger over my lip and let it slide down my neck, over my breasts, down my stomach and straight into my pussy.

"Cum for your man Sommer." I lifted my leg up and gave him access to go deeper.

"Yea Sommer. Just like that. You sexy as hell."

"Percyyyyyy." I yelled and my body shook in his arms.

"Sommer, you need to thank me."

"I do right." I stripped him out his clothes and took him in my mouth.

"Fuck my mouth Percy."

"Oh shit Sommer. You know I love when you talk shit." He pumped fast and then slow in my mouth until he came.

"I want some dick Percy."

"Then do you." I sat on top and fucked the hell out of my fiancé. We heard someone knock on the door and Percy told them to come back later.

"Yes, oooh yesssss." Percy and I had been in this office for a long time and both of us were exhausted but neither of us wanted to be the first to tap out.

"Let's cum together Percy." He fucked me faster from the back and both of us exploded and fell on the ground.

"Your office is officially christened."

"Thanks babe. I love you."

"Anything for you Sommer." He pulled me up, we put our clothes on and opened the door. After we took turns going in the bathroom, he had Carol call the chick in.

"Hi. Carol said you wanted to see me." She said to Percy with a smile on her face. She didn't see me standing on the side.

"Yes, we did." I startled her and she grabbed her chest.

"Marissa, I'm going to cut to the chase. My husband is off limits and if I ever see you staring, coming on to him or even attempting to flirt, after I beat your ass, I'm going to fire you."

"I'm sorry. I didn't know you were married."

"Honey, it's not your business if we're married or not. We came in together, holding hands and kissing. We may have just been fuck buddies but you were disrespectful as hell lusting over him in front of me. He had to stop me from jumping on you."

"I didn't know."

"You're not listening. If a man arrives with a woman, unless he tells you otherwise, assume she is his woman. I'd advise it, if you want to stay out of shit. Not every woman will be as calm as me. Now, I don't want to have this discussion again and I suggest you inform all the waitresses here as well. I don't play when it comes to him and a bitch will lose her life fucking with me." Percy was shaking his head.

"It won't happen again and thank you for not firing me." She refused to even look at Percy and walked out.

"You can't be threatening people babe." He walked up on me and wrapped his arms on my waist.

"What are you going to do about it?"

"Do I need to have you running from this dick again?"

"Whatever." I couldn't debate what he said because he dug so deep when he hit it from the back, I did run a few times.

"Can we have dinner now?"

"I guess." I closed the door and went to have a nice quiet meal with my man.

****

"Mrs. Johnson, is there a reason you don't want to be married to this man?" The judge asked as we stood in divorce court. I filed a motion a couple days after Kevin ruined my baby shower and today was the day to hopefully have it finalized.

"Your honor, Mr. Johnson and I were married at a young age and in the beginning, I was in love with him. However, he became very abusive and even engaged in many affairs."

"Ma'am there's no paperwork on abuse allegations."

"I was afraid and never filed. I do have all the hospital visits and even though he wasn't the known perpetrator, I can say he was."

"Mrs. Johnson, I'm sorry but I can't even look at the paperwork if he wasn't named." Kevin looked over and smiled. I wanted to shoot him in the face.

"I understand. If I can continue?" I asked and he nodded.

"Mr. Johnson was incarcerated and I tried on various occasions to divorce him."

"What happened?" He looked at me with his glasses on the brim of his nose.

"The presiding judge at the time told me because he was incarcerated and Mr. Johnson wanted to work on our marriage, he wouldn't grant it." He removed his glasses.

"And did it work?"

"No sir. I received tons of threatening letters from Mr. Johnson while incarcerated. I reported it and the jail stopped him from sending me anymore. Judge, I'm all for marriage and this it isn't something I take lightly. However, he is very violent towards me and over the last six months he's sent me more threatening messages, along with staking out my house, following me and the list goes on and on."

"Did she tell you how she had a baby with another man while we're still married." Kevin shouted out and the judge stared at him and smirked.

"Mr. Johnson, you'll have your turn to speak." Kevin had an attitude.

"Is there anything else Mrs. Johnson?"

"No sir. I just want to move on with my life and he won't let me." He nodded and asked Kevin what he had to say. This motherfucker had the nerve to break down crying and shit. If I could've taken a picture I would have. He told the judge he was in hell without me, while in prison. When the judge asked about the women he cheated with and even the one who was in the car with him when arrested, all he came up with is, she was a friend.

"Well it looks like this entire marriage has been a sham from the start and I can't even attempt to understand why the previous judge didn't grant this sooner. I'm ready to rule." I turned to look at my parents who came with me.

"Wait!" Kevin yelled out and asked if he could take some papers up. The judge sent the bailiff to get them and chuckled when he looked. I had no idea what they were but I was curious.

"Mrs. Johnson will you and Mr. Johnson rise?" We both stood up. The door opened and Charlotte stepped in with a smile on her face.

"Hello, Miss Charlotte. I'm shocked to see you here." The judge said and she waved him off.

"In the case of Johnson vs. Johnson, I hereby grant the divorce on grounds of irreconcilable differences. I am also putting a permanent restraining order in place against you Mr. Johnson for terroristic threats and stalking."

"WHAT?" He yelled and the bailiff made a call on his radio. It's the best because when this fool gets mad, it's a problem.

"Mr. Johnson, you need to calm down."

"Fuck that. What about her money? She is rich and I want alimony." My mouth hit the floor when he said that shit.

"Mr. Johnson, if you let me finish, I'll tell you." He seemed to start calming down and turned to look at Charlotte with a grin on his face.

"Mrs. Johnson, after going over your bank statement and the paystubs from your job, I order you to pay Mr. Johnson here five hundred dollars every two weeks for the next two years."

"That's not shit."

"Mr. Johnson, you have been out of jail for six months and have you even tried to get a job?"

"Get a job for what? My wife is rich."

"Ex-wife and per my pay stubs and bank account, five hundred dollars is all I can afford to pay you. I have to live too Kevin." I blinked a few times with a grin on my face. My father had someone erase my name from any bank accounts I had because we knew for a fact, he'd try to take my money.

"What about the pictures I gave you? She is committing adultery and.-" The judge showed me photos of Percy and I kissing. Where the hell did he get those?

"All these photos show is you are stalking this woman, which is why the restraining order is in place. Mr. Johnson, if I were you, I'd get a job and steer clear of Miss Dawson."

"FUCK THIS SHIT. I'M COMING FOR.-"

"KEVIN!" Charlotte yelled out and he listened. All of us gave them a crazy look.

"Good day judge and bitch have my checks sent to my mom's house like you did everything else." He stuck his finger up and walked out. What a big ass fucking baby. The judge concluded the session and directed one of the guards to walk me to my car.

"You ok Sommer?" Susie asked and gave me a hug.

"I'm fine and glad it's over with. I can't wait to tell Percy."

"Where is he?" My father glanced around the courtroom.

"I didn't tell him because he would've probably killed Kevin." We all agreed and started walking out. I opened the door to leave and heard my name being called.

"I'm going to get you bitch." Kevin yelled and the officer called for backup. I shook my head at the attempts Kevin was going through.

"Anyway, where are you two going?"

"I'm about to make love to my wife until she can't take anymore." Susie smacked him in the arm. I was happy she finally took him back and he was too. I gave them a hug and they waited for me to get in my car before pulling off. My phone started ringing and before I could answer, I heard her.

"Take your perfect patty ass to the warehouse and tell me if your life is still perfect when you see what your nigga hiding, dumb bitch." Charlotte yelled out as her and Kevin pulled off in the same car, I peeped them in that night at the gas station. I ignored her and called Percy back. He never answered so I took my ass home.

My daughter was excited to see me when I entered the house and so was Percy Jr. I couldn't help but think about what Charlotte said though. It brought me back to when she mentioned it before. How does she even know what Percy has going on in the warehouse? What is really going on?

I called Percy a second time and once again, he didn't answer, which now had me nervous. He didn't tell me about any special meetings he had and if he were cheating, I swear, I'm never fucking with him again and I mean it. I told the

96

nanny I'd be back later and drove to this so-called warehouse. I've never been here and it looks different seeing it in the day time.

I parked, stepped out my car and made my way to the door. One of the security guards who work at the club sometimes, was there too. He gave me a hug and opened the door for me. The person working the inside gave me a crazy look but the dude told him to allow me access. He shrugged and pressed a button to open the door, which led me to another door. I walked in and it seemed like a regular warehouse. Men were on forklifts moving shit and others were walking around with clipboards. It didn't appear to be any foul shit going on. I noticed a few offices upstairs and made my way there.

I started to see women, which did make me feel a tinge of jealousy because they were bad and dressed in business attire. Don't get me fucked up now, I had on an all black, Tom Ford business suit, with a pair of Jimmy Choos and my Celine bag in my hand. My hair was perfect and my face was beat as usual. I guess when you see competition, the intimidation sets right in. Each one spoke and smiled, which gave me the assumption, they knew exactly who I was.

"Hey. Percy know you here?" My new-found brother Robert asked. I hadn't seen him much since we found out but we spoke and texted on the phone a lot.

"No, I wanted to surprise him. I have some good news and I wanted to tell him in person."

"Oh. He's going to be surprised." He had me follow him to another hallway. The doors were steel and it only held two huge offices with glass windows to see in.

"Mr. Miller. Your wife is here?" Robert said as he knocked on the door. He opened it and a bitch almost lost it.

# Percy

When Robert opened the door and I peeped my soon to be wife, I knew shit was about to go left. Sommer dropped her purse and Millie stood up and smiled. She was being smart but this wasn't going to go in her favor and she figured it out too late. My girl already had her on the ground banging her head into it. At first, I thought about stopping it but let Sommer continue because this is what she gets.

Before everyone starts to go off, Millie is the chick who I fucked a few times in Cuba when Sommer and I weren't speaking. She started talking about how she fell in love, so I left her alone. I told her never to contact me again and as you can see she didn't listen.

When Sommer and I got back together, I informed her and she knew who Millie was from the photos she sent to my phone. Some were of her dressed and others were naked, hence, why I blocked her. My ass was not about to deal with Sommer cutting me off. I lost her once and refused to lose her again.

The reason Millie was in my office is because she claimed to have had information about Hector coming over to the states. It had me wondering how she even knew where the warehouse was. However, if she came here with so called news about him, he may have told her. Millie was only here all of five minutes before Sommer came, but when my girl walked in, she saw this dumb bitch trying to kiss me, which is why she got her ass beat.

"That's enough babe." I pulled her off and Robert stood there laughing. The nigga had the nerve to call Jaime in here. Now I had two assholes watching and cracking jokes.

"Why is she here?" Sommer started fixing her clothes. I had to move her because she kicked Millie in the face a few more times.

"Yea. Why she here Percy?" Jaime loved starting shit.

"Yo. Get somebody to get this bitch out of here."

"Why you yelling at little ole me?" Jaime was about to make me fuck him up. He knew it too because he ran out laughing.

"Babe, she got here this morning and before you ask. I don't know how she found this place."

"Hmph."

"I hate when you do that shit. Say what's on your mind."

"If you don't know, then someone sent her. Check and make sure she doesn't have a wire." I smiled. My girl was on point.

"Already on it but I love how you peeped game." I pulled her in front of me and squeezed her ass.

"Damn baby. This suit is too tight and you showing my ass to niggas." I squeezed it again. Her ass wasn't huge but it was enough to make niggas turn heads when they saw her. I hated and loved it at the same time.

"Mr. Miller, you asked for a removal?" A chick came in and smiled.

"Hi, Mrs. Miller. I didn't know you were here." She extended her hand to shake.

"How are you?"

101

"Boss, you didn't do her any justice." She stared at Sommer.

"Yo, T.M. Back the fuck up. My wife is off limits." Sommer put her head down blushing.

"I would never. But she is bad boss." She stood in front of my girl.

"Let me know if he cheats. I swear, I'll kick his ass and then make you happy." She winked and I jumped at her.

"I'm playing. Anyway, this problem will be cleaned up shortly. However, now that your wife is here, I think we can finally get rid of the other one." I nodded and told her to have security open the door. She and I spoke for a few more minutes and she left.

"Percy, how does everyone know who I am?" She questioned.

"Your photo is on my desk, and even though you never come here, you're in the system to gain access whenever you want."

"Oh ok." She seemed happy about that.

"Babe, I'm about to show you something. I've been waiting for you to be ready and I think it's time."

"Percy, this office is nicer than mine. I think it should be christened too." She ran her hand under my shirt.

"I got you later babe." We stepped over Millie and left out the room. I opened a steel door that led to an elevator. She stepped on in front of me and turned around with a smirk on her face.

"Babe, if there weren't any cameras, I promise, I'd fuck the shit out of you on here. And hell no, we won't do it anyway. You're my wife and no other nigga will see any of your body."

"Can't they turn them off?"

"Stop being a brat." She grabbed my shirt after I pressed the elevator to go down.

"The judge granted my divorce." I backed up and stared to see if she was playing.

"Word." She nodded her head up and down with a big ass grin on her face.

"He had to put a permanent restraining order in place because Kevin started cutting up."

"WHAT? Sommer why didn't you tell me about this?" I grabbed her hand as we stepped off and went down another long hallway.

"You've been busy lately and I can't take the chance of you flipping out in court. Then I'd have to find a new man to keep me warm at night." I tossed her against the wall.

"Don't ever play those games with me."

"Ooooooh, I'm saying that later. Look how mad you got. I know if we were home you'd tear me up." I had to laugh at her crazy ass.

"Percy, I've been meaning to ask. How does Charlotte know what you have going on in here?"

"What you mean?" She started telling me the only reason she came is because of the comment Charlotte made. I wondered why she showed up because she never came here but then again it didn't matter. I wasn't hiding shit.

"Your nosy ass mother saw me put this bitch in my car one day. I wish you would've asked me earlier about it."

"Ask about who?" I opened the door and she stared at me.

"You still with this bitch?" Chrissy yelled out.

She was tied to a chair and has been since she was caught trying to run Sommer off the road. See, I knew the type of bitch Chrissy was and made sure I had someone keep a close eye on her. The night I almost killed my baby mother and she came to the jail starting more shit, she followed Sommer.

I knew my girl was upset and probably wouldn't pay attention to her surroundings so I put someone on her. Come to find out, Chrissy began following her and was about to hit the back of Sommer's car, which would have pushed her in oncoming traffic and possibly killed her. I couldn't have that and had Chrissy picked up and brought here. Dreek told me to get rid of her a long time ago but I saved her for Sommer.

"He sure is. My husband ain't going nowhere but you are." She picked the gun up off the table and pointed it her. All of a sudden Chrissy started begging for her life.

"What about my son?"

"That's my son bitch."

*POW!* Chrissy's head was splattered against the wall. I asked Sommer why didn't she whoop her ass first? She told me this was overdue and it she would've gotten on her nerves as they fought. Sommer was on some other shit and I loved it. Oh, my girl was definitely getting fucked tonight.

****

"See you made it back safe nigga." I said to Dreek when he came to my house. He went to Cuba and set shit off.

"You already know. What up with you though? Jaime called and told me Sommer was at the warehouse." I started telling him what happened when the doorbell rang again.

I let the nanny answer it and heard her call for Sommer. I didn't think anything of it until I heard someone say bring your ass outside. Dreek and I ran to the door and Sommer was coming down the steps at the same time.

"JIAO!" All of us yelled out at the same time. None of us have seen or heard from her.

"What's up J?" Sommer moved closer and Jiao punched her in the face. Neither Dreek or I moved, as the two of them started fighting. The nanny stared at me. I shrugged my shoulders and went back in the living room. Dreek stayed but I think it was more or less to see Jiao in general. His ass was missing her something serious and we all knew it.

Five minutes went by and no one came in the room. I went to check and both of them were holding each other's throats. I figured it was enough time to get that shit out the way and started pulling them apart. Neither of them wanted to let the other go, so Dreek grabbed Jiao roughly and carried her out the house. Of course, she was screaming for him to get the fuck off of her.

"Relax baby." I shut the door and checked her over.

"Fuck that Percy. How she gonna come here and.-"

"You deserved it Sommer."

"What?" I shrugged my shoulders and walked away.

"Percy."

"Sommer, you deserved it and we all know it." She stood there.

"Jiao may not have told you shit about Hector at first but when the shit hit the fan and she tried to call and tell you, you ignored her. Then she ended up getting shot and was in the hospital for three days. Not to mention, she's up to something

107

with Hector and he tossed her out of a moving truck." She had tears coming down her face.

"Jiao has gone crazy but not in a mental way. She killed Queenie, burned down Mandy's house and there's no telling what else she has done. The most fucked up part about you not being there for her, is when she found out her father is the one who got her mother killed, and you weren't around to comfort her."

"I didn't know."

"You asked me if I thought you were wrong and I told you, if I were her, I wouldn't fuck with you and I mean it. You are the only person Jiao had left besides her son and you left her hanging. I love you Sommer but you foul as hell for that."

"I thought she was going to have you killed."

"So, what if she were? As your man, you're supposed to have my back, I get it. However, as her friend, it was up to you to hear her, instead of shut her out."

"I fucked up babe." She slid down the wall crying. I sat next to her and she rested her head on my shoulder.

"She's never going to forgive me."

"Give her time. If she didn't want to, trust she wouldn't have come here. You two needed to get that out of the way first." She nodded and after a few more minutes I carried her upstairs. These two are crazy.

# Dreek

"Calm your little ass down Jiao before I fuck you up." I told her after carrying her out the house and putting her in my car. I had to eventually place her in the back seat with the child safety locks because she kept trying to get out and we needed to talk.

"Fuck you Dreek. Let me go." She kept kicking the back of my seat. I ended up pulling over and snatching her ass out. Luckily, we were at the house already since this place isn't far from Percy.

"Go in the house." She stood there.

"Fuck you."

"FUCK ME J! Really." I shouted.

"Damn right fuck you. Get the fuck off my property." She said and went in the house.

"I ain't going no fucking where and this is our property." Her and the kids were staying in the house I brought for us. The one she fucked up is the old one I been had and never got rid of.

"Just go." I shut the door.

"Where are my kids?"

"Does it matter? You haven't been around them." I grabbed her wrists and held them tight.

"I'm always around my son and Dree when you're not. Don't think because you don't see me with them, I'm neglecting my kids. Your mouth is about to get you fucked up." I let go and she punched me in the face. She knew she fucked up too because she backed away and had a terrified look on her face. It took everything in me not to hit her. I rubbed my temples and kept telling myself, she's angry about how I left her at the warehouse.

"Jiao, I promised I wouldn't hurt you but if you put your hands on me again, I can't say I won't fuck you up."

"Go ahead and hit me Dreek. It won't hurt any more than you leaving me in a warzone." I ran up on her and grab her shirt.

"I left you but I swear on my pops, you were protected."

"How Dreek, huh? You had a fucking laser on my chest and I was shot." I chuckled.

"I would never allow a man to even pull a gun out around you, unless it was necessary. You think I would let one of my men put a fucking laser on you?"

"But you did."

"Jiao, listen to yourself. The laser was on you as soon as I got close. Hector is the one who had the laser. Why do you think I said take them all out? I couldn't take the chance of you standing there explaining your involvement and they kill you. Yes, I was hurt and wrong for walking away but it had to happen. If I stayed there and they killed you, trying to get me, I would've never forgiven myself. I didn't expect you to run after me and it's the reason you were hit. The person watching you, ran behind you and got lost in the dark. When I found out you were hit, he was dead."

"It doesn't explain why you didn't let me tell you how I knew him."

"I don't give a fuck how you know him Jiao and I'm not even mad you didn't mention your involvement. I'm mad because you brought your ass out to a warehouse at night. What were you thinking?"

"Dreek you didn't come home and I called over and over. I thought something happened to you." I saw she was getting upset.

"Jiao, I'm sorry for that. Mandy came in the club and started telling me she was your ex best friend and you were holding secrets. I was on my way home and she shot me in the bathroom." She covered her mouth.

"I woke up in the hospital and went to check on Queenie because I remembered her texting me she gave birth. I go in the room and another nigga holding the kid. If that's not bad enough, imagine my surprise, as I'm sitting at the warehouse watching you on fucking video with my got damn enemy in your face."

"Then you saw me smack him."

"Once I peeped y'all, I grabbed my gun and came for you. I didn't know what was going on." She didn't say anything.

"Jiao, I hadn't even been up from surgery a full twenty-four hours and I still made it my business to make sure you were good."

"Dreek."

"No J. Before we walked out the warehouse, I told every nigga in there to make sure you were not in harm's way. I should've been the one protecting you J, but I didn't have the strength. I swear, I'm sorry for that." She started crying.

"I lost my fucking mind when Jaime told me you were hit. It took a bunch of niggas to keep me in the warehouse and not come to you in the hospital that night."

"You knew where I was."

"Of course I did. Jiao, I've always had someone on you, why don't you believe me? I know what you did to Queenie and how you let that punk nigga go." She wiped her eyes.

"I will never let anyone hurt you Jiao."

"Why didn't you come Dreek? I didn't wake up for three days and you were the only one I wanted to see. I prayed you call or text me but there was nothing." I nodded.

"I did come. I watched you sleep for hours. I left you balloons and flowers in your room. If you paid attention you would have known. The day you were released, I left and went to Cuba."

"To fuck the bitch you been sleeping with right." She stood up and went upstairs. I tried to stop her but she snatched her arm away. I started to leave but we weren't finished talking.

"Jiao." She had just taken her shirt off and was on her way to the bathroom.

"What the fuck happened to you?"

"I'm fine Dreek."

"This isn't fine." I pointed to the bone that appeared to be sticking out her side. She walked in the bathroom and turned the shower on.

"When Hector tossed me out the truck, I had some crack ribs and because I didn't sit my ass still, some didn't heal correctly." She shrugged and stepped in the shower. All she did was add more fuel to the fire of how I'm going to torture the shit out of him.

I walked out the bathroom and waited for her to come out the shower. All I could think of was how I failed to keep her safe after I made that promise and it was fucking with me. Her knowing about the shit with Sabrina came straight from Hector. His bitch ass couldn't wait to fill her in. Bash told me she wasn't happy about it and I'm sure it's fucking with her too.

She came out and started drying off. She's never been shy around me when it came to her body. Most women would cover up or throw their clothes on in the bathroom but not her. I watched her lotion up and put her pajamas on. I pulled my phone out and text Percy to tell him we had to meet up and get Hector before shit gets worse. I only did it to keep my eyes off her because my dick was rising and sex wasn't an option right now.

"Dreek." She stood in front of me and lifted my head to look at her. Jiao was beautiful to me and staring at her now, is like staring at her for the first time. Everything about her was perfect, even down to the bone that didn't heal.

"Yea." She sat on my lap and wrapped her arms around my neck.

"I'm sorry."

"Jiao.-" Her tongue invaded my mouth and it was nothing left to say. I had her stand in front of me as I undressed her again.

"Damn." Her pussy was shaved perfectly and she lifted her leg on my lap. I took my shirt off and felt my phone going off. I'm sure its Percy texting me back.

"Yessssss. Oh Gawd, I missed you." Her head was back with her hand on my head. I had two fingers inside playing with her g-spot as my tongue snaked in and out of her.

"Right there Dreek. Shit." She started shaking and my phone went off again.

"Baby, I'm cumming." I held on to her so she wouldn't fall and waited for her to catch her breath. My phone went off again.

"WHAT?" I yelled in the phone without looking at the caller.

"Baby, I miss you." Jiao heard and jumped off me.

"Get the fuck off my line yo." I hung up and placed my phone on the dresser. Jiao was grabbing her pants to put on and I snatched them right out her hand.

"Dreek." I lifted her up and sat her on top of the dresser, spread her legs open and unbuckled my jeans. It wasn't the real tall dresser but the medium size one, with the mirror that came with bedroom sets.

"Give it to me Andreek." She scooted closer to the edge of the dresser and I forced myself in.

I didn't have time to be gentle. My dick craved her and right now it was all I needed to fulfill what my body ached for. She pulled my face to hers and kissed me hard and aggressive. What we were doing wasn't making love or fucking. The animalistic aggression we had towards one another was nothing like we've ever done before.

"Turn over."

"Dreek, this dresser is small and I'm going to fall."

"I got you." She smiled and did what I asked. Her ass was in my face and my dick was at her entrance.

"It's going to hurt." She and I spoke about doing this but today is the first time we're trying it. I've never done it and she's the only woman I'd ever consider it with anyway.

"Shitttttt Dreek." She moaned and her face was pressed against the mirror.

"I'm almost in. You want me to stop." I didn't go any further until she answered.

"No baby." I pushed further and a nigga fell deeper in love. Her ass was virgin tight and the way it felt squeezing my dick, had me lost.

"Look at me Jiao." I grabbed her by the hair with one hand and used my other one to massage her clit, that was extremely hard. I placed a kiss on her back and smiled when she looked in the mirror.

"Oh, shit baby. It's hot and, oh fuckkkkk." She started throwing her ass back and my nut came up so fast, I couldn't hold it in, even if I tried.

"Ahhhhhh damn baby." She fell back on me. We had both cum together and the experience was fucking amazing, if I say so myself.

"Hold on J." She wanted to get off the dresser but I had to pull out slow. I didn't want to hurt her. She turned around and tried to stand. The shit was funny as hell as she held her ass cheeks together.

"Come on." I carried her in the bathroom.

"Get in with me." I did like she asked and watched her bathe both of us. Once she finished, she stared at me. The water was beating down her face but I could still see her tears.

"Why are you crying?"

"I love you so much Dreek and I don't know what we're doing but I don't want you to leave."

"Jiao.-"

"You have unfinished business with that woman and I don't want or need anymore drama in my life. Dreek.-" I stopped her.

"I get it J and no woman will ever come before you or my kids. I love you too and want the same things but you're right. I have to deal with some shit and I don't want you caught up." She turned the shower off and we both stepped out.

"Can I ask you something?" I started putting my clothes on.

"What's up?"

"Do you love her?" I stopped and stared at her.

"Jiao Kim, you are the only woman who has my heart. I know it sounds cliché but baby, no one can take your spot and that's some real shit. You see how hard it was for you to get it. Do you really think I have the time to fall for another woman? Plus, your ass ain't about to let another bitch get this." I put my wife beater on and pulled her close. She smirked and sucked her teeth but she knew I wasn't lying. Jiao would not allow me to be happy with another chick and we both knew it.

"Why did you have to sleep with her? Now she's calling and.-" My phone started ringing again.

"Answer my phone J, tell the bitch you're my wife and stop calling." She looked at me crazy. No woman answers my phone and she knows I flip out if one even touches it. I wanted to show her how much she meant to me.

"Dreek, it's not necessary and if she gets smart."

"She will." Jiao smirked and told me to hand her the phone. She definitely be on her petty shit too. I picked the blunt up she had on the nightstand and lit it.

"Hello." She answered and looked at me. I had her sit on my lap so I could hear the conversation too.

"Where the fuck is my man?" I could hear Sabrina yelling.

"Your man. Honey, Dreek has one woman and you're speaking to her." I smiled and pecked her lips.

"Oh, this must be the Chinese chick."

"So, you know about me." Jiao stood up.

"Yup, and It means nothing because he was still fucking me."

"Notice how you said was. His wife is home and it's in your best interest to lose his number." I lifted her pajama shirt and kissed her stomach.

"I'm putting another baby in here when I come back." I told her.

"Sabrina, I have to go because our man wants me to have another baby."

"WHAT?"

"Oh, I guess he doesn't want the same thing with you. I guess he's mine after all. Bye bitch." Jiao hung up and stared at me.

"Get rid of her. When I decide to take you back, no bitch should be claiming you." I grabbed her wrist.

"It doesn't matter who claims me. I'm only claiming you, remember that." I smacked her on the ass and passed her the blunt.

"I'll see you later." I stood to leave and watched her lay on the bed.

"Lock up." She put the blunt out and rolled over.

"If you want me to stay, say it."

"Nope." I hated when she did this spoiled shit.

"Jiao, I'm not coming back out if I bounce." She shrugged her shoulders and never turned around. I walked out the room, the house and sat in my car. I thought about going back in but fuck it. She has to open up to me, the same way she wants me to open up to her.

# Jiao

When Dreek left, I laid in the bed mad as hell. Of course, I wanted him to stay but I wasn't going to say it because he already claimed I'm spoiled. People can say what they want but I missed my man and he may have left but you can bet, I'm going to get him. It was late but the time meant nothing to me when all I wanted was him.

I rolled out the bed, threw some clothes on and hopped in my truck. I didn't even know where he was staying, since I fucked his house up and hadn't spoken to him until today. I drove by his mom's and his car wasn't there. I kept going and stopped in front of his old place and parked next to his. The light was on in his room but the rest were out. I used my key and went in. I was shocked he didn't change the locks but then again, he wasn't worried about shit.

"Sabrina, I told you weeks ago I wasn't fucking with you. That's my woman and if you disrespect her again, I'll be on the next flight and it won't be for the reason you think." I heard him say as I opened his bedroom door. I didn't say

124

anything as he sat on his bed with just a pair of boxers on. I stripped out my clothes and crawled on it.

"Damn bae." I placed kisses on his legs and moved up his thighs and then to my favorite part of his body.

"Bye Sabrina. Don't hit my phone again." He hung up and I heard it hit the floor.

"Ssssss. Got damn J." He moaned out. I spit on the tip and let my hands go up and down his shaft in a massaging way. I put my mouth low enough to take his balls in and swish them around like pieces of candy.

"Yea J." He sat up to watch like he always did and bit down on his lip. He knew that shit turned me on.

"Fuckkkk." I put my mouth back on his dick and went up and down fast. His dick started twitching and I tasted the pre-cum. He swelled up more and a few seconds later, I swallowed like my life depended on it. I loved tasting his sperm. Call me nasty but I'll be that for him.

"Get your nasty ass up here." He had me put my pussy on his face but in a sixty-nine position. He and I went at it, pleasing one another. I can't even count how many times he made me cum.

"Sit on your man's dick." He had me ride him cowgirl style and a bitch damn near passed out after he hit me with a deadly stroke. My body shook violently, unlike ever before. He put me on all fours and did the same.

"Jiao, you are my woman and whether we live together or not, you are all I want." He had my hair pushed to the side as he sucked on the back of my neck. He grabbed my hips, dug deeper and went in circles. I swear, he was marking his territory.

"You hear me Jiao?" He pulled out and pounded me harder.

"Yesssss. Dreek, there's no one else baby."

"It better not be and you're getting off birth control."

"Ok. Baby, right there. Oh shit, here I cummmmmm." I started breathing heavy but Dreek wouldn't let me tap out.

"Nah baby. I missed this pussy." He had me get off the bed and bend over to touch my ankles. I thought he was about to give me the D but he put his face in and gave me more

126

orgasms. I can tell you right now, my ass is going to sleep so fucking good tonight.

"You like this Jiao?" He stuck his finger in and I came again.

"I know you tired J. Make me cum so we can go to sleep." He said. I had him sit on the floor with his back against the bed, climbed on top, stood on my feet and rode the fuck out of him. He sucked on my breasts as I bounced up and down harder and faster. I slowed down and his arms were under mine, holding my shoulders as we continued fucking each other in this positon.

"Arghhhhhh damnnnnnn." He shouted out. His body twitched and he came so hard it took him a few minutes to calm down.

"I fucking love you Jiao Kim. You're going to be my wife." I pulled my face out his neck and stared at him.

"I know we started off trying to kill each other but I swear you're my soul mate J. You're the only woman I wanna wake up and go to bed with. I love everything about you and there's not a woman out here who can compare to you. Marry me J." I covered my mouth and let the tears fall down my face. He wiped them away and reached under the bed.

"Dreek." He opened the box and there sat an ocean blue diamond sitting in it. I can't tell you how big the diamond is, but know when he slid it on, it went from the bottom of my finger to almost touching my knuckle.

"I didn't hear you." He looked at me.

"Yes, baby yes." I kissed him over a hundred times on his face and lips. I put my hand out and stared at the ring. It was beautiful and I couldn't wait to show his mom and Dree.

"Jiao, I know we're dealing with some shit but I won't cheat on you. I need for you to trust me at all times. I will never lie to you." I nodded.

"Dreek, you are the only man I want to be with and if you tell me to trust you, I will. You've always kept it real with me from the very beginning and I don't expect you to change. I want to apologize for punching you."

"J."

"No, it's not ok Dreek. Domestic violence is what it is, whether you see it that way or not. I don't want Dree or lil

Dreek ever seeing us lay hands on one another. Your mom told me what you went through and I damn sure don't want our son to grow up and have the same mentality." He raised his eyebrow.

"I'm sure you'll teach him right from wrong with women but I never want them witnessing it from us." He put his hand behind my head.

"I could never hurt you Jiao. The times I did, I felt you deserved it but I would never do it again. I love you."

"I love you too." We kissed one another deeply and he stood to walk us in the bathroom. Yea, I was still attached to him and I damn sure had my ring on. This time he washed us up. I admired how he broke down his walls and poured his heart out. It was probably hard but he did it for me and I planned on doing it for him.

****

"Wake up Jiao." I heard and had to put my finger in my ear to clean it out. I know damn well this bitch wasn't here.

"Jiao, I know you hear me." She said and I sucked my teeth. I turned over and Dreek was standing there smiling.

129

"Give her a minute to get dressed Sommer." She nodded and stepped out the room.

"Morning bae." He moved the covers off me and licked his lips.

"Not right now babe. My pussy is swollen."

"Awww. Let me kiss it." He put his face down there and kissed it like he said and my body reacted. I opened my legs and he started laughing.

"When she leaves." I rolled my eyes. He took my hand and came in the bathroom with me. He stood behind me as I brushed my teeth.

"I love looking at you. Jiao, you are beautiful." I smiled and toothpaste dripped out my mouth.

"Awwww." I spit the toothpaste out and pecked his lips.

"Put some clothes on before I forget you said you were sore." He grabbed his dick.

"I have to shower first and why are you up and ready?" I turned the water on.

"Percy called and asked if I heard from you. He said Sommer wanted to talk to you and he was bringing her over.

Lucky for you, I didn't wake you up until they got here, so you owe me." His finger was not massaging my clit as I stood in the shower trying to wash up.

"Got dammit Dreek." He pulled me away from the water and kissed me.

"Mmmmm." I came and watched him lick his fingers.

"I love the way you taste. Now hurry up." He left me standing in the shower, weak.

I came out and he already changed the sheets and blankets. My clothes were laid out and my slippers were on the side of the bed. I can't believe he still had my things here. I figured all of our shit was in the new house but I guess he never took everything. It made me think about all the fucked-up shit I did to this place. He must've had someone come in to clean it because I know his ass damn sure didn't.

I rubbed lotion on and started putting my clothes on when his phone rang again. I picked it up and the caller was unknown. I wasn't worried about him getting angry if I answered. He only reacted that way with the ho's he slept with; especially when he thought I called. He and I had a long talk

131

last night about everything. He explained who Sabrina was, the shit he did in Cuba and I broke down and told him what my father did. I'm sure he knew but he still let me vent. Dreek has a side to him that no other woman will probably ever see, that I loved.

"Hello." I answered and when the person remained silent, I knew it was a woman.

"This is Dreek's phone so if you want to speak to him, you may as well say hello." I laughed in the phone as I put my jeans on.

"Where the fuck is he?" I looked at the phone.

"Mandy, is that you?"

"Yea bitch and why are you answering his phone. He's about to snap and I hope he fucks you up."

"Oh, you think he will. Hold on. DREEK!" I yelled out and waited for him to come up.

"You ok." I handed him the phone.

"Yea. One of your ho's is calling. She wants to know why I answered and she's waiting for you to beat my ass like you did her when she touched your phone."

132

"Yo, who the fuck is this?"

"Mandy. Why you calling my phone and questioning my girl. She can answer my phone, my door and anything else she wants to. The fuck type of shit you on?" I laughed and put my shirt on.

"Man, go head. Don't think I forgot you shot me. I'm coming for you but I need to get my wife pregnant first." He hung up and stared at me.

"I didn't say a word."

"You better not. Get your sexy ass over here." He pulled my belt loop. I wrapped my arms around his neck.

"I meant what I said Jiao. My seeds better start planting soon."

"They probably already started."

"Why you say that?"

"I haven't taken birth control since that night." He lifted me up.

"Let's get married next month."

"I'm ready when you are." He said and carried me on his back down the steps to deal with this chick.

133

"Be nice." He whispered in my ear and left us in the kitchen.

# Sommer

I woke up this morning feeling uneasy about the situation with Jiao and I. Yes, we argued a lot over the years but we've never come to blows the way we did last night. I listened to Percy explain how fucked up of a person I was for over reacting about the Hector shit. None of us gave her a chance to explain and it wasn't fair to her.

She tried to call me and I refused her calls. When he told me what went down with her father, I really felt like shit for not being there for her. What type of friend turns her back? All I could do is try and make up with her and if isn't something she wants to do, I have to accept it.

Dreek had her on his back when they came down the steps and the smile on her face, showed how happy she is. Hell, I've never seen Dreek smile as much as he was either. God put them together for a reason and I'm happy to see it working out for them.

He put her down and she stepped in the kitchen. I walked in and sat at the island as she opened the tray of food

Percy and I picked up for them. Dreek only agreed to allow us over here this early if we treated them to breakfast.

"What do you want Sommer?" She starting off nasty but I deserve it.

"I'm sorry Jiao. My emotions were all over the place when Mandy shouted the shit out and all I thought about was Percy dying."

"So, fuck me. I've been your friend all my life and you turn your back on me for a man." I went to speak but she stopped me.

"I love Dreek with all my heart and hell no, I don't want anything to happen to him, but if some shit came out about you supposedly setting him up, guess what? I'm calling you out on it. I want to know why and what was the purpose. I'm not going to keep sending you to voicemail or even ignoring your calls."

"J, I didn't know and you have to see it from my point."

"How fucking dare you sit here in my face and tell me I should see it from your point? I know how it looked and I wanted to tell everyone but all of you left me. You treated me

136

like I was a fucking disease Sommer. I had no one. NO ONE!" She yelled out.

"And you fucking left me to stand on my own. I could've died and you abandoned me like our friendship meant nothing."

"Jiao, I understand."

"DO YOU SOMMER?" She started shouting again.

"Dreek didn't have two words for me and I get it. He had every right to turn his back on me. Granted, he didn't let me explain but I wasn't as mad at him, as I was with you. I laid in the hospital for three fucking days and when I woke up, no one was there for me, not even my own father. Did you know Hector tossed me out of a fucking moving van because he wanted to fuck me and I yelled out Dreek's name. I was NAKED Sommer." She wiped her eyes.

"Again, I had no one. I find out about my dad and watched him die in front of me and you weren't there for that either."

"I should've been." I was now wiping my own tears.

"Guess what Sommer? You are a piece of shit and I'll never forgive you for it."

"Jiao."

"GET THE FUCK OUT MY FIANCE'S HOUSE."

"FIANCE?" I questioned.

"Yes, fiancé and no bitch, you're not invited to the wedding."

"JIAO." Dreek barked and she jumped.

"Hey baby. Sommer was just leaving. Hey Percy." She picked her fork up and started eating again.

"Let me talk to you J." Percy said and took her outside.

"What should I do Dreek?"

"I don't know. I told your ass you were foul and so did Percy. You wanted to pretend you didn't give a fuck. How did you expect her to react?" He picked up a piece of bacon out Jiao's tray to eat.

"I said I was sorry."

"Sorry don't make up for missing out on important shit she went through."

"Why isn't she mad at you?"

"First off Sommer, our situations are different. You two grew up together. Second... I had every right to be mad because the plot was against me. Also, Jiao may have been on a rampage but she was always protected. It may have seemed like I turned my back on her but I never did. Whatever she needed, she got. My family and friends had her back and so did Bash, the one person who we'd all expect to hate her. He was there for her when I was out of the country. You were in town and not once did you check on her. That why she's so fucked up over it."

"I wanna fix it but I don't know how."

"Give her time. When she's ready, she'll talk. Shit, when she was ready to fight, her ass showed up, didn't she?" We both laughed as her and Percy came in.

"I'm ready Percy and Jiao, I apologize from the bottom of my heart for turning my back on you. You know my number when you want to talk and I promise to answer, no matter what time it is." She walked over to Dreek, wrapped her arms around him and kept her face hidden in his chest. I didn't know what else to do but I can say, I tried. Percy opened the door for me and we left.

"You good?"

"Yea. I can't expect her just to forgive me."

"Nah you can't. She misses your friendship too babe but she's really hurt."

"I tried apologizing."

"But you did it when you felt like it, not when it should have been done. Therefore, you have to wait until she's ready to accept it." I nodded and listened to him talk on the phone for the rest of the ride home.

****

Two weeks went by and I still hadn't heard from Jiao. Percy told me Dreek did indeed propose and she wanted to get married the following month. He told her all she had to do was give him a time and he'd show up. I was really happy for her and kicked myself in the ass for being stupid. I was missing another important moment she may have needed me and this time it was because she didn't want me there.

Percy had been to the tailor twice already to get his tux ready and I had no idea what colors they were even wearing. I was scared to ask if I could go, but he would've told me no if that were the case. Plus, I don't see my man attending without me but then again, Dreek's his best friend and he wouldn't miss it.

I walked around the mall going from store to store looking for an outfit to wear to the wedding. I picked out a nice peach dress and took it in the dressing room to try on. I was about to remove my shirt but stopped when I heard a voice. Ever since the judge had me paying his broke ass every two weeks the five hundred dollars, he stopped bothering me.

I peeked out the dressing room and he stood there holding Mandy's hand. I wanted to beat her ass for Jiao but I couldn't risk Kevin attacking me. We all know a restraining order ain't shit but a piece of paper. It won't stop a crazy motherfucker. The crazy thing is, Kevin stalking me for money is not because he wants to be with me. I believe he's doing it to have a reason to be on contact with me of some sort, even if it's through me sending checks.

141

My dad ended up hiring a private investigator to follow my mom. She was for sure an informant for the feds and so was Kevin. Both of them were only out of jail because of the deals they made. What I couldn't understand was who Kevin thought he could tell on. My father kicked him off the team a long time ago and Percy would never attempt to hook him up.

"Where is it Sommer?" I tried to leave the store without anyone seeing, but it didn't work out that way. I turned around and saw Charlotte standing there staring at me. I tried to leave but she blocked the door. Kevin had an evil grin on his face and once Mandy noticed me, I knew shit was about to be on.

"I don't know what you're talking about." I pushed past her and all three of them were behind me talking shit. I sped up and pulled my phone out to send a text to Percy. He text right back and said someone was on the way and not to walk out of the mall. I went into a sneaker store because men worked in there and hopefully, if Kevin tried anything they would help.

"I'm not going to ask again Sommer. Where is it?"

"Charlotte, can you leave me alone?" I tried to remain calm. She pushed me in the back. I turned around and punched her in the face.

"Oh shit yo." I heard one of the workers say.

"Bitch, where is the fucking USB and paperwork?" Kevin had his hands around my throat and my body was dangling in the air.

"Let me go Kevin." I felt my body becoming weak. I looked over and the workers, along with Mandy and Charlotte were staring at me. The workers were scared as hell and I could tell because they weren't recording and their eyes were big. Kevin is not a small dude. He was 6'3 and all muscle. Those poor boys wouldn't be able to do shit.

"Your nigga aint here to save you now."

"Nah, but her brother is." Robert hit him so hard, he hit the ground, sleep. Him and Jaime started fucking Kevin up. Charlotte and Mandy were both screaming. I had no remorse and once I caught my breath, I fucked Charlotte up.

"Break it up." Security was now in the store as well as cops. The scene was chaotic and it took some time for shit to calm down.

"You ok." Percy came running in with Dreek and some other guys. They were wheeling Kevin out on a stretcher.

"Yea. He choked me and.-"

"He what?" Percy had a scary look on his face. He lifted my head to examine my neck. Dreek and one of the other guys had to hold him back.

"Go to the hospital and make sure he doesn't leave." He told Jaime who I already knew was probably going to kill him.

"I want her arrested for attacking me." Charlotte pointed to me and the cops looked at Dreek who nodded his head no.

"Ma'am we have to view the tapes to see what transpired. If she indeed attacked you, we will take it from there. Right now, you and your lady friend need to exit the mall." The cop told her and she walked out talking all kinds of shit. Little did she know, I had plans for her ass and I'm

handling it soon.

# Dreek

I wanted to murder Mandy's ass right there in the mall but there's a time and place for everything. I noticed her smile at me and switch going out the store. The sad part is, she'll let me fuck if I want, thinking my ass forgot all about the shooting. I'm going to let her think it's over and catch her slipping.

"You good?" I asked Percy while we were walking to the car.

"Yea. Let me get her home. You know what's up later." I nodded and made my way to the car.

"Yea J." I answered in the phone.

"Dreek, I'm only going to ask so don't think I'm accusing you." I lit a blunt and pulled off.

"Shoot."

"Were you with Mandy?"

"You can say that." I looked down on my phone because I heard the beeps and my screensaver was showing of her and the kids. She took a selfie of them and sent it to me, so I saved it on my phone.

"Why you hang up?" She hung up again.

How she say she not accusing me and when I answer the question, she hangs up? I drove to the house, knowing I have other shit to do because I hated to argue and since I know what's about to happen, I may as well get it over with.

I parked in the driveway and stepped out the car. I could hear the music blasting, which meant she was most likely cleaning. It's what she did faithfully on Saturdays. I opened the door and she had on some black compression shorts with one of my wife beaters and some flip flops wiping down the coffee tables in the living room. She had her back turned and probably didn't know I was there.

"You sexy as hell." She jumped and pushed me away from her.

"Go back to your side chick." She tried to walk away and I grabbed her.

"You're my wife, my side chick, my mistress, my girlfriend and my freak. I don't need to fill those spots when you have them all." She smiled and removed her wife beater.

147

She unstrapped her bra, lifted her breasts and juggled them trying to be smart.

"Suck on them for me baby." I licked my lips.

"Nah, I want you to suck my dick for the bullshit you just pulled." Now it was her turn to lick her lips.

"Why you treating me like a ho?" She asked and undid my belt and then my button.

"If my man finds out I'm giving you what he only receives, he will kill both of us." I felt her pull my boxers down and watched her stroke me.

"Damn baby, you are well endowed. I'm not sure I can handle all that." My dick was harder than shit listening to her roll play like she wasn't my chick.

"Most bitches can't. Let me see if you can." Her mouth opened wide, she slid me inside and went to work on me.

"Dreek, I know I'm not your woman but can I taste you?" I smirked.

"My girl may get mad and I can't have. Oh shit woman.-" She was now jerking me off and licking under my balls.

"Ahhhhhh damn J." I released what I had inside and enjoyed the sight of her being the one doing it.

"I guess you have to go now." My phone started ringing and I handed it to her.

"What Mandy?" She answered and I leaned her over the couch, removed her shorts and spread her ass cheeks open.

"He can't come to the phone because he's making love to his wifeeeeeee. Oh, my gawdddddd Dreeeeeek." She dropped the phone when my tongue slid in her ass. She started throwing her ass back on my face like it was my dick. I smacked her cheeks and then began squeezing them.

"I love you so much babyyyyyyy. Uhhhhhhh." She moaned out and cum started spitting out her pussy.

"I know. Let daddy fuck you real good before I head back out." She stayed leaning over the couch, which made me start fucking the shit out of her. Her ass was jiggling and her hands were gripping the couch. I bit down on her shoulder and watched her body shutter.

"Whose pussy is this Jiao Puryear?" I hit her with my last name even though we weren't married yet.

"Yours Andreek Puryear. Fuckkkkk." She came again and again.

"Ride your man." I pulled out and walked in the kitchen and had her ride me on one of the chairs. I wasn't about to mess our couches up.

"Yea baby. Just like that. Fuck J." I looked at her pussy swallowing my dick as she rode me and became even harder.

"Got damn baby girl. Shit, here I cum."

"Me too Dreek. Ahhhhhhhh yessssss." She screamed out and I came at the same time.

"I need a nap." She said and put her face in the crook of my neck.

"Daddy put that ass to sleep again huh?"

"Always baby. Do you have to go back out?" She asked as I carried her upstairs.

"Why?" Usually we'd get in the shower but right now, we were lying in the bed.

"I wanted you to lay here with me. You know I don't sleep well when you're not around."

"I got you." She laid on my chest and both of us fell asleep.

****

"Where you at nigga?" Jaime barked in my phone. I looked at the time and it was damn near six o clock. J wasn't in the bed.

"I fell asleep."

"Still making up with your girl huh?"

"You already know. What up?"

"Oh, we handled that already so you don't have to come." I knew he was speaking of Kevin and I'm happy they did because a nigga still tired.

"Alright, I'll see you tomorrow at the rehearsal shit."

"You know damn well I ain't missing this wedding for no one. The chick to get your sexaholic ass to calm down, is worth listening to." I laughed at his dumb ass, threw some shorts on and went downstairs to see what J was doing. I smelled food and saw the kids in the kitchen with her. I gave them a kiss on the cheek and walked over to her. She turned around and wrapped her arms around my neck.

"I had to get the kids. Your mom was going on a date as she says."

"You good."

"Mmmm. You still have me on your face and breath baby. Go clean up."

"How you know I don't want to keep it there?"

"You can but then the kids can't play with you." I busted out laughing.

"I'll be back in a few minutes." I left them in in the kitchen and cleaned myself up.

****

"Damn bro. I can't believe you're taking the walk down the aisle next week." Percy said as we sat outside the 7-11 talking. Jiao and Dree greedy ass wanted a damn Slurpee. He met me over here to ask if Jiao was ok with Sommer attending the wedding. I told him she hasn't said no, so bring her as my guest.

"Still sexy as ever." I turned around and it was Mandy. I yanked the bitch up by her throat and threw her on the ground.

152

"I'm sorry for shooting you Dreek. I just wanted you to be my man. I deserve you, not that fucking ho." I kicked her in the stomach and was about to hit her again.

"Were you whooping her ass like this when you found out she fucked my cousin after you left her at the warehouse?" I grabbed her up by the hair.

"What the fuck are you talking about?"

"Let's go Dreek. You know she stay talking shit."

"It's true. Hector said it's the reason he tossed her out the truck. They were fucking and she called out your name."

"Let's go Dreek. Too many people are starting to come."

"I'm out yo. I got something for your ass too Mandy." I jumped in my car and sped all the way home.

"Calm down bro." Percy followed me here and out of nowhere Jaime popped up. These niggas be on me when it comes to Jiao. I opened the front door and she was in the living room with the kids watching television.

"Hey baby. Where's our Slurpee's?"

"Go upstairs Dree."

153

"What did she do? Dreek what's wrong?" Concern was written all over Jiao's face.

"NOW!" I yelled out and they both jumped.

"I'll be up there in a minute Dree. Go ahead so I can find out what's wrong with daddy." She waited for Dree to close the door before she spoke.

"Why are you so upset and don't speak to her like that."

"First off, don't tell me how to speak to my daughter."

"Excuse me!" I didn't mean to say that to her and I could tell she was offended and hurt.

"I'm going to ask you something and I swear you better not lie."

"Whatever it is, ask me another time because I have to check on your daughter." She attempted to go upstairs.

"Did you fuck Hector?" She froze and without saying a word, I knew she did. I put my hands on top of my head to keep them from around her neck.

"I'm not going to ask you again." She came towards me with glassy eyes.

"Dreek." She reached out for me.

154

"Don't fucking touch me. You ain't shit but a ho just like the rest of these bitches." I saw tears cascade down her face. She was hurt but so was I.

"Can y'all excuse us for a minute?" She asked and they looked at me.

"Jiao, I love you like a sister but leaving you alone with him is not an option." Percy told her and he was right. I promised never to hurt her again but it hurt too bad for me, not to want to.

"Fine. I'll say what I need to and you can take him out of here." She wiped her face.

"I didn't plan on having sex with him Dreek." My fist balled up and my feet started moving towards her. Jaime and Percy stood in front of me.

"He snatched me out the restaurant and forced me in his truck. I fought to get out and he threatened me. I had no choice."

"Did he rape you?"

"No." I would have rather her told me yes.

"Then you enjoyed it."

"Dreek, it wasn't what you think and.-"

"It wasn't what I think." I was now in her face.

"Did he stick his fucking dick in you?" She didn't answer.

"DID HE?" I yelled and she dropped to the ground crying harder.

"Yes. But I yelled out your name, which is why he tossed me out the truck." I guess she thought saying that would make me feel better.

"So, you're telling me, you allowed him to fuck you but I should be ok with it because you were thinking of me."

"I would never expect you to be ok with it. Just like I'm not ok with you running off to Cuba to fuck you side bitch or whoever she is. I'm not ok with you telling me I shouldn't have done what I needed to stay alive. I'm not ok with you screaming out she's your daughter when I'm the one helping you fucking raise her and I'm not ok with you verbally attacking me because you found out another nigga smelled my pussy." She had me feeling bad all the way up until she said that.

"You let him go down on you too." My chest was going in and out and I think she knew what was coming because she hopped up off the ground fast as hell and moved away from me.

"Calm down bro. Jiao, go upstairs and don't come out."

"There won't be a marriage." I yelled and she turned around.

"Dreek, come on." Jaime said and I stared at Jiao crying.

"I can't walk down the aisle with a ho. A woman who slept with the enemy and never once thought to tell me."

"Andreek."

"Don't say my fucking name J." I headed to the door.

"I get that you claim to do what you had to, I do but the fact you couldn't tell me this shit on your own, don't sit right with me. We spoke about everything when we got back together and not one time did you mention this. I can't help but wonder what else you're holding in. Jiao, I swear to God, I love you to death but I can't marry you. I'm out yo." I walked out the door and straight to my car.

"DREEK! DREEK! Don't leave me again. Please. I'm sorry." She was banging on my window hysterically.

"DREEK!" Jaime pulled her back and I sped out the driveway. I'm not going to front, I had to wipe the few tears from my own eyes. She had me weak and right now, it's not something I can be; especially with Hector lurking.

# Mandy

I finally got through to Dreek when it came to Jiao. I saw the hurt and anger on his face when I yelled out his precious woman fucked someone else. Granted, Hector told me he wasn't even in longer than a minute when she called out Dreek's name but I wasn't telling Dreek that. Let him think my cousin had her in all kinds of positions. I know how much it bothers niggas when they hear their woman is the one cheating. They can't handle shit the way a woman can. It eats away at them and I knew it would destroy their relationship.

Jiao has always said she would never give her virginity up to anyone, unless it was her husband. I knew when she started messing with Dreek, she had to have strong feelings for him to allow him close to her. J has never been the type of chick to flaunt herself around guys but they always seemed to flock to her. Instead of fucking them, she became close with all of them and they'd to this day, still have her back if needed. Sometimes I wish we had the friendship we use but it wasn't in our cards.

"Hello." I answered.

"Why didn't you tell me about this fucking marriage?" Hector yelled in the phone and I had no idea who he was speaking of.

"What are you talking about?" I started stripping out my clothes to jump in the shower. Dreek fucked my stomach up when he kicked me and all I wanted to do is soak in a hot bath.

"Dreek and Jiao are supposed to get married next week." I reached for the knob and turned the water on.

"I wouldn't worry about it."

"Why is that?"

"Because I just informed Mr. Dreek himself of you and Jiao's sexual encounter and he wasn't too happy."

"Oh yea. What happened?" I explained to him what went down and he couldn't stop laughing.

"You did good cousin and I'm going to send you something to your account. Check in about five minutes." He hung up and I laid back in the tub reminiscing on the way

Dreek used to fuck me. I began playing with my clit and moaning out loud. *Shit!* The release was well needed.

I washed up, drained the tub and stepped out. My phone started ringing again and shockingly it was Samantha. I hadn't heard from her in a long time. She called herself going off on me about Brandon and Dreek. I wasn't going to answer but why not? I needed a good laugh.

"Yea Samantha."

"You busy?"

"No. What's up?"

"I came by your house and I see it's no longer there."

"You trying to be funny."

"No. I was asking because bitch I'm standing here with Percy and Dreek." My ears perked up.

"Why are you with them?"

"Well, I'm not with them but we're outside the store and I want to fuck Percy but he may not be down. I know if you get with Dreek, he'll roll with it."

"Girl Dreek ain't fucking with me right now."

161

"What? He just asked me where you were because he just finished having it out with his girl and needed to fuck, his words, not mine. Now you already know I'll fuck him if you don't want to. However, Percy looking like a snack too."

"Bitch, you better not touch my man. Where you at? I'm on the way." She gave me the address and I started getting dressed. I heard my phone ringing again on my way out the door.

"Where you at yo? We fucking or not?" Dreek barked in the phone and my panties instantly got wet. Say what you want, but when good dick calls, you go running.

"I'm coming baby."

"Hurry up." I jumped in my car and headed to where they were.

It was packed out here and I didn't see them anywhere. I sent him a text and ask where he was. When he mentioned the hotel waiting for me, I sped out the fucking parking lot. I basically ran in the hotel and to the third floor. I knocked on the door and he stood there looking sexy as fuck.

"I missed you Dreek." I hugged him and he let me.

"What you miss?" He leaned on the dresser where the television was.

"All of this." I tried to unbuckle his jeans and he stopped me.

"Get naked." I did like he asked and kept my eyes on him the entire time.

I couldn't tell if he was turned on by my body because the light wasn't on and he blocked the TV. My stomach had some pain in it, but I gave no fucks right now because I was about to get exactly what I've been waiting for.

"Mandy, why did you tell me that shit about Jiao and your cousin?" He had me get on my knees on the bed.

"I thought you should know. I knew you would be upset but I didn't want her playing you. You're too good of a man for that." He smiled and let his hand run through my hair.

"I am right."

"Yes baby." He tilted my head back and I felt his breath on my neck.

"Too good for you to have contacted your cousin and let him know too." My eyes opened wide when I felt the grip become tighter on my hair.

"Dreek, he called me." He snatched me off the bed and drug me across the floor. My back was burning from the rug.

"You want to be Jiao so bad, you're willing to do anything to get me."

"I love you Dreek." He opened another door to the suite we were in and Samantha came out with a grin on her face and so did my sons father Brandon.

"What the fuck?"

"How does it feel to know I'll be your son's mother when you die?" She smacked the shit out of me.

"What? He's married?" Brandon tossed his head back laughing.

"May I Dreek?" Brandon asked and Dreek dropped me on the floor.

"Samantha has been my girl for years Mandy."

"WHAT?"

"You were so wrapped up in being a ho, that you never took the time out to realize the woman taking care of our son, is the only woman I loved. You tried to ruin it when we were younger and it took me a hell of a time to win her back but she was worth it." He's calling me a ho, I wonder if he knows his girl sucked Dreek's dick?

"But how?" I was confused as hell right now as to what was taking place.

"Have you ever met my so-called wife?"

"No. I mean we met once when we almost fought."

"No stupid. You met a woman, who we paid to pretend she was the wife. Had you done your research, you'd know it was Samantha's cousin who lived in Delaware. You never met her but she has quite a bit of photos at Samantha's parents. Anyway, here's what's going to happen." I started putting my clothes on and listened to him talk shit. The entire time Dreek had his eyes on me and not in a good way.

"My son barely knows you and thinks Samantha is his mom already."

"You ain't shit."

"You're right but you knew that when you fucked me."

"I would hate to be you right now." Samantha said with a grin on her face.

"I don't know what you did to Dreek but you know as well as I, that once you get on his bad side, that's it. The only reason I'm here is to watch my girl take your life."

"Say what?"

"You heard me. It's the only way I know for sure you won't try to come for my son again." I turned around and Samantha had a gun pointed at me.

"Wait! I'm pregnant." They all busted out laughing.

"Please don't kill me."

"I've been waiting for this moment for years." Samantha said and pulled the trigger. I guess I was the most hated person in the world.

# Jiao

"You should've told him J." His mom said as I sat inside her kitchen crying. It was the day I was supposed to marry the man of my dreams and I hadn't even spoken to him. I know he's been handling shit with the guys but I wanted him back.

"I didn't know how to. Hector didn't rape me but in order for me to get the device in his truck, I had to stay. It may not have been the right thing to do and honestly, I didn't expect Hector to try anything." She sat down in front of me and handed me a glass of soda.

"Jiao, I understand you want to get Hector but you sold your soul to do it."

"What you mean?"

"You gave him a piece of you that only Dreek was supposed to have." I raised my eyebrow.

"Listen. I'm not saying my son is perfect because Lord knows he's not. However, you have never been touched by anyone but him. To allow another man to touch you in order to get a damn tracker put in his truck, is plain stupid."

"I know."

"I could see if you and Dreek were broken up for a while and you found someone else. You are entitled to sleep with him but come on Jiao. You even let him eat your pussy and didn't use a condom." I put my head down in shame. At the time, everything went down with Hector it didn't seem as bad as it does now when I hear it.

"He loves you Jiao and I'm not saying he won't get over it but you need to have more respect for your pussy." I lifted my head.

"You can have an attitude all you want missy but it's the truth. Men can sling dicks all day long. Women are held to a different standard and even though its bullshit, it is what it is."

"Ma, where you at?" My heart started beating fast when I heard his voice. I'm sure he didn't know I was here because my truck was in the garage. I stayed here last night with the kids. I didn't want to wake up alone on my, would be wedding day.

"In here boy and why you yelling."

"I'll see you later." I stood up and turned around to see him standing there looking good as ever.

"Um, excuse me." I said and moved the hair behind my ear. I was hurt and nervous to be around him. He didn't say anything, nor did he move.

"Daddy." Dree yelled out and he finally moved to pick her up. I walked out the door and to my truck.

I let the garage door open and pulled out without as much as peeking to see if he were checking for me. I drove to the only place I knew would give me comfort right now. I pulled a blanket out my truck, grabbed my beats pill and walked to my mom's grave. Like always, I checked Dree's mom to make sure her area was straight before I went to see my mom. I laid the blanket down, turned the pill on and laid on my back.

"I messed up mommy. Today is my wedding day but my boyfriend found out I did something bad and called it off. I wish I could take back the day in question but I can't. I thought I was doing the right thing. It turns out the right thing in my eyes, was the wrong thing in everyone else's." *God what did you have to take my mommy?*

I turned over on my stomach and let the tears fall from my eyes. I cried for my mom, my father, even though he got my mom killed, and I cried for Dreek. He was all I had left as far as being close with someone and now he's gone. I have no idea how long I was out here but when I woke up it was dark and Sommer was next to me.

"Dreek's mom called and said you left the house and no one has heard from you."

"Not that anyone care's."

"Jiao, I'm so sorry for leaving you in the wind. I wanted to call you a hundred times but I thought you were setting Percy up. What if I made a call to you and someone traced it to me. I had my daughter to think about and Percy's son. I should've known you wouldn't do that. But Jiao, you never even told me about Hector or that you did hits for my father. It seemed like you were holding in secrets and I couldn't help but be protective of my family. I apologize a thousand times sis." When she called me that I broke down crying again? I missed her. We ended up hugging for a good five minutes.

"I was going to invite you to the wedding but.-" I shrugged my shoulders and she asked me what happened. I guess her and Percy didn't pillow talk about everything.

"Jiao, you were wrong. Your pussy is yours and free to give away to who you choose but I have to take Dreek's side on this. How would you feel if he let a bitch suck his dick or ride him to do the same thing?"

"The crazy part is, he did."

"Huh?"

"He flew to Cuba after he left me at the warehouse and fucked the chick he had been sleeping with. He stayed there for a few days, which ain't no telling how many times they fucked. And this happened way before he found out about Hector."

"Oh shit, he foul too then."

"No one sees it that way because he wasn't a virgin or a female. You know they go by the double standard shit." I wiped my nose with my hand.

"Don't I know it."

"Anyway, I forgave him for it because he was upset too. He broke down and told me everything Sommer but I couldn't find the words to tell him about Hector. I knew he would react the way he did. I never want him to hurt and I know it sounds crazy because of the shit we went through but he is my everything."

"And you are his Jiao's." She stopped and looked around.

"Evidently, Mandy is the one who told him."

"That bitch."

"Yea well. She assumed it would get him in bed with her."

"And did it?"

"Nope. He had the chick Samantha call her up and she made it seem like he wanted her. He lured her to the room and was about to kill her but Samantha did it instead for fucking

Brandon all those years ago. Do you know they were a couple and she's been raising Mandy's son?"

"Get the fuck out of here?" She started explaining the shit Percy told her and I must say it sounded crazy.

"That's what her ass gets. I don't feel sorry for her." Sommer's phone went off and she showed me a text from Percy.

**Percy:** *Tell me you found her so I can let this psycho nigga know. He's getting on my fucking nerves right now.*

We both laughed and I had her tell him she didn't find me. Let Dreek's ass worry about me the same way I worry about him. He hadn't called to check on me the whole week but when I go missing, all of a sudden, he wants to make sure I'm ok. I had her call Dreek's mom up and tell her I'd contact her tomorrow. All I wanted to do tonight was go home, shower and go to bed.

"Call me in the morning so we can go to breakfast." Sommer yelled as she pulled off.

I headed in the direction of my house. When I got there, I locked up and showered. I went in my closet and pulled the

173

wedding dress out I had custom made and flown in from France. The shit was expensive as fuck but well worth the money. I kept it in the plastic, held it to my chest and busted out crying.

"Nice dress." Dreek said and walked in the room. When the fuck did he get here? I wiped my eyes and put the dress back in the closet.

"Well, I'm donating it tomorrow." He shrugged his shoulders and walked around the room checking shit.

"Ain't no nigga in here." I climbed in my bed.

"You ain't that stupid but then again." He raised his eyebrow at me.

"Get the fuck out. I'm not in the fucking mood to argue with you."

"I'll be gone in a minute." He continued looking for something so I went down to the kitchen to grab a water.

"Found what you needed I hope." He came down the steps and stopped in front of me.

"I'm out yo." He put up his two fingers and opened the front door.

I shook my head and went to my room. I didn't even bother to turn around and I don't know if the door was even locked. I climbed back in my bed and turned the television on. The BET Awards were on again and I could never get enough of watching the Newedition tribute. My phone went off and I didn't bother to look at it until it went off two more times.

**Sommer:** *He misses you J.* She sent me a photo of her standing behind him and looking on his phone of our picture. She must've taken it earlier.

**Me:** *He just left here and didn't say two words. He can't be missing me too much. Goodnight.* I placed my phone on the nightstand and laid there until sleep found me.

****

The next day, I woke up with a whole new outlook on life. Today, I was going to the lawyer's office to have all of my father's restaurants and laundromats sold. I didn't want any parts of his businesses. It's the reason I lost both my parents in the first place. It's like the longer they were around, the more of a burden they were.

I threw on some ripped jeans, a short sweater and a pair of Jordan's to match. I called up Dreek's mom and told her I was on my way to get the kids. We were going shopping after the lawyers' office and I planned on renting a room, so Dree and I could go swimming. There was a pool in the back yard but it was chilly out. The hotel had indoor ones and plus lil Dreek would have a ball too. I sent Sommer a text to tell her where we would be so she could bring her kids too.

"Hey lil man." I picked my son up and he slobbed all over my face. He was definitely his father's child when it came to looks. I'm one of those women who just carried my son because he had not one of my features.

"Dree, you ready?" I yelled up the steps and she came down fully dressed and I could see her bathing suit under her shirt.

"Nana has a big mouth. It was supposed to be a surprise." I spoke of the fact we were going swimming.

"Whatever heffa. Am I telling my son where you are?"

"Why would you do that? He hasn't been looking for me."

"I'm staying out of it." She put her hands up in surrender and laughed.

"Anyway, the kids and I are going to Disneyworld next month. Do you want to come?"

"We are. Yea." Dree became very excited. I came up with the idea last night. I felt like we needed to get away from here and have family time with just us.

"I sure do. Let me know what the days are."

"You got it." I headed out the front door and put the kids in the car.

We ran around all day and by the time we got to the hotel both of the kids were exhausted. I opened the door to the room and Dree instantly started taking her clothes off and asking for the pool. I guess she wasn't that tired.

I couldn't keep her in the room so I went to the truck and took my son stroller out. I would lay him in it while we played in the pool until he woke up. I made sure I had his bottle and swimsuit ready for when he woke up.

It was a few people in the pool but not too crowded. Shockingly, there was music playing. It wasn't my type. At least it wasn't super quiet in here. Dree started to put her floaties on her arm and asked me for help. Those things are hard as hell to pull up her arm. She put a small donut float around her body and jumped in the pool and started splashing everywhere.

The few kids in there saw her and made their way over. In less than five minutes, kids were screaming and splashing one another. I took my jeans and shirt off and caught the lifeguard staring at me with his mouth open. I laughed and dove in the pool head first, only to come out the water and stare straight in his face.

# Dreek

When my mom told me Jiao came and took the kids swimming, I was low key mad, I missed her. I planned on hearing her out last night but when I went to the house, she had an attitude. I felt like shit walking in the room and she had the wedding dress against her body. Yea, I called if off, however, it didn't make me feel any better seeing her crying so much. Jiao loves me, I know, unfortunately, the shit Mandy told me should have come from my girl and not anyone else.

I drove to the hotel I knew she was at and parked in the lot. It was the only one who had an indoor pool. I watched Jiao go in the truck and retrieve my sons' stroller and take it inside. Most likely he was asleep and she was leaving him in there. I waited for her to go in and finished my blunt before I did the same.

When I opened the door, a smile came on my face as I watched Jiao remove her clothes and show off her body. She wore a black two-piece bikini and her chest almost spilled out

179

the top and her ass was perfect in the bottom. I wanted to kill the lifeguard on duty. I swear the nigga had a hard on staring.

"Don't make me push you off the fucking chair and drown your ass bro."

"Huh?"

"Don't huh me. That's my fucking wife you drooling over." He closed his mouth and turned his head. I stared at Jiao as she rose up. The water was coming down her face, her hair was drenched and her body was bad as hell. I snapped a picture before she could tell me no.

"What are you doing here?" She pulled the suit out her ass and walked up the steps. I wrapped a towel around her and made sure no one was looking.

"Dreek, what are you doing?"

"It's too many motherfuckers in here staring at you." She stopped and looked at me.

"Are you serious."

"Hell motherfucking yea, I'm serious." She shook her head and kept walking.

"What do you want?"

180

"I went to see the kids and.-"

"Your mother talks too damn much. I told her not to tell you."

"I'll make sure to tell her that."

"You better not." She picked my son up who started crying and I took him from her.

"You're wet J. He ain't felt the water yet so it's going to be cold on him." She sat down in the chair and kept her eye on Dree in the water.

"I'm ready to hear what you have to say." I told her and threw my sons diaper in the trash. I took his shirt off and put his shorts on. His greedy ass wanted to eat.

"I'm not talking about anything right now." She removed the towel and I almost lost it.

"Put the fucking towel on Jiao."

"Dreek, this is a damn pool. Why would I wear a towel?"

"Then put a shirt on over it." She sat up on the lounge chair, opened her legs and leaned back on the chair. Her pussy looked fat and I felt my man bricking the fuck up. She had a smirk on her face, which meant she was doing the shit on purpose.

"I swear J."

"You swear what Dreek?" She stood in front of me and the water from her body started falling on me.

"You play too much." I shook my head and burped my son.

"I'm not paying you no mind." She walked away and went back in the water. She grabbed Dree and started playing with her. They were splashing and she tossed Dree over a few times and she loved that shit.

"I see your ass couldn't leave sis alone." Jaime said walking in with his on and off again girlfriend. Then I saw Cameron, Bash, Sommer, Percy and their kids, along with Robert and some chick.

"What the fuck yo. Why all y'all here?"

"Nigga, this ain't your pool." Jaime said and had his chick sit down.

"Yea nigga." Robert co-signed.

"Oh, my goodness. Give me my nephew." Cameron snatched lil Dreek from me and started putting kisses all over his face.

"All of you have rooms here?" I asked and they each held up a key.

"Y'all petty as fuck."

"Who is that getting out the water? Damn, yo."

"Jaime, I swear to God, I'll break your fucking neck if you don't stop playing with me." They all thought the shit was funny.

"Aye yo. Cover your ass up." Now he was yelling at his girl who had on a two piece and she had a nice body too.

"Nah bro. Let us all look." Jaime was like the fucking devil snapping his head back when I said it.

"Oh, it ain't funny now, is it nigga."

"Fuck you."

"Let's go Jiao." I grabbed her hand and asked my brother and Cameron to watch the kids.

"What Dreek?" She opened the door to the hotel.

"Tell me why you did it?" She stood there with her arms folded.

"It doesn't matter. I understand why you were angry. I should've come up with a different plan and I'm sorry." I lifted her face.

"Do you have feelings for him?"

"Absolutely not. It was a bad decision and I did it to place a tracker in his truck. It was the only way to get close to him. It was dumb." I untied the top and back of her bathing suit and let it fall on the ground. I made her step out the bottom and had her spin around.

"Damn, you sexy." She blushed. I took my sweats off and lifted her up.

"I just need a feel baby." I told her and forced myself in like always. I had her on the table with her legs wide open.

"Dreek."

"Yea babe."

"I hate you."

"I know. Let me see how much you hate me." I pumped harder inside and she tried to throw her pussy back but it was no use. I stayed in the room fucking the shit out of Jiao.

"Ahhhh damn J. I'm cumming." I hated when she squeezed her muscles on my dick. It always made me cum fast. I knew she did it on purpose. I fell on top of her, laid my head on her chest and listened to her heart.

"I'm sorry Jiao for leaving you." She had her hand rubbing my head.

"I have to work on not blowing up and leaving when shit gets rough but I didn't cheat on you. I stayed with Percy and Sommer the whole time."

"She didn't even tell me."

"Just like she didn't tell me you were at the cemetery for hours."

"How did you know?"

"Someone is always watching you. I had Percy ask to see if she would tell him. When she didn't, I knew the two of you made up and she was covering for you." I lifted Jiao up and walked in the shower. After we finished, I put my clothes on and she put on a one-piece bathing suit she had, we walked back to where the pool was. It still showed off too much of her body if you ask me.

"Why did you come by last night and what were you looking for?"

"I came by just to lay eyes on you and to find this." I stopped her and put the ring back on her finger.

"Where did you find it?" She only took it off when she showered. I took it the day I found out about Hector to have a guard put on it because she said it kept sliding off but she still wore it.

"I had a guard put on it. I had the ring but I wanted to put it in the box." I kept the box in my dresser but I couldn't let her see me take it out the drawer. That's why when she went downstairs it was a good thing. I was able to grab it and leave.

"Are you sure Dreek?"

"Do you have any more secrets?" She stood there thinking and it pissed me off.

"I don't think so. Dreek, the only reason I didn't mention it, is because I knew how you would react. I hated to

186

see you hurting over it and I regret not telling you. I'm sorry but you are the only man I'll ever want." We started kissing.

"I better be." She smiled and we walked in the pool area where everyone was.

"Damn sis. This bathing suit looks better than the other one. Shit girl." I pushed Jaime's ass in the pool. He played too much.

"That's not nice."

"Neither is him or any man looking at my wife."

"Dreek, we're not married."

"Don't worry about that. You're my wife and it's all I'm going to say."

"Jiao, aunty Cameron isn't throwing me in the water right. Can you show her?" Cameron looked offended at Dree.

"Hold on." J took the towel off and walked to the pool and I swear my dick got hard again.

"Sooooo, is the wedding back on?" Jaime asked dripping wet.

"Yea. I need her as my wife ASAP."

"Good. You were getting on everyone's fucking nerves, pouting and shit." Robert said and went to get in the pool.

"What? You were." Percy said and followed him to get in. Sommer had their daughter in the water and Percy Jr. was being tossed by Bash.

"You getting in babe?"

"Nah. If I do, I may fuck you in the water."

"Who says I don't want that?"

"Jiao, you play all day."

"Come on." She pulled my arm and I told her I had to get my shorts out the car.

"Hey baby." I heard. When I looked, I had to take a double look. How the fuck did Sabrina get here?

# Jiao

I watched everyone in the pool splashing and having a good time. Who would have known a day in the pool with me and the kids, would turn into the whole crew coming along? I'm not complaining because these are the only people I'm cool with and will be my family soon.

The way the guys were with their women made me look around for Dreek. He walked out ten minutes ago saying he had to get his shorts from the car. I asked Percy to keep an eye on the kids while I went to find Dreek. Just like I expected, Sommer stepped out the pool to follow me and so did Cameron, Jaime's girl Bridget and Robert's friend; I think her name is Carrie. It's funny how we knew nothing but were all onto something.

"Who the fuck is that bitch?" Bridget said and started wrapping her hair up with a hair tie from her wrist. I met her a few times and her personality was the shit. She didn't play when it came to Jaime but you can tell she had some ratchetness in her. Carrie, who is Robert's friend seemed

189

standoffish the few times we met but something about her screamed ghetto.

"If I had to take a guess, I'd say the bitch Sabrina from Cuba."

"CUBA!" They all shouted at the same time.

"Yup. She has been stalking the shit out of Dreek. I know this because I've answered the phone and she's in denial of him not wanting her. The text messages are beyond crazy and explicit of course."

"I bet they are. Bitches kill me when a nigga tell them to beat it. They swear a picture of their pussy or a video of them cumming will keep him." We all looked at Carrie.

"What? Robert and I have been exclusive for two months now and one of his fuck buddies can't take a hint. The bitch had the nerve to send him a video of her playing with a dildo and cumming as she moaned his name. I ain't knocking her but if he ain't your man, then you shouldn't be sending it."

"I know that's right?" Cameron said.

"What you wanna do?" I didn't answer and pushed the door open with them in tow.

"Sabrina." She turned around. Dreek shook his head and stepped away from his car.

"Babe." I held my hand up for him to stop talking.

"I got this babe." He smirked and stepped back.

"This is a long time coming."

"If it isn't the Chinese B.-" I punched her in the face and she fell against the car.

"I see my man telling you no hasn't registered." She smiled.

"Dreek and I have been fucking around for quite some time now and your little blasian ass think you can take him away from me. Honey, you are sadly mistaken." This bitch pulled a gun out on me and Dreek lost it on her. He banged her head into his window and broke her nose. Blood shot everywhere. Why this bitch thought she could come for me without repercussions is beyond me.

"That's enough babe. I want to finish enjoying our day." I told him and grabbed his arm. I was shocked my voice calmed him down.

"Bridget do me a favor and tell Jaime I said we need someone to clean the parking lot." We all knew what it meant.

"You ok?" He asked and stared in my eyes.

"Oh boy. They're about to kiss and probably fuck on his car." Cameron said and we both laughed.

"I'm gone." Sommer left.

"Me too. The only porno I'm watching, is with me and my man." Carrie left and we were the only two standing there.

"No one will ever hurt you."

"I know baby. It does feel good to know that even when you're upset with me, you're still watching."

"Always. Now come on before I do bend your ass over this car." He grabbed my hand and I kicked Sabrina in the face before we went in.

"Overkill J."

"Who cares?"

"Can't take you two violent motherfuckers nowhere." Jaime yelled and I smacked him in the chest.

"Stop cussing in front of the kids."

"My bad. I'm sorry Dree and PJ." That's what he called Percy Jr.

"Its ok cousin Jaime. I hear daddy cuss a lot when him and J are in the room and I'm supposed to be sleep."

"Damn, she throwing it on you like that Dreek." Robert asked and I wanted to laugh but I couldn't. I took her hand and made her take a walk with me.

"Dree, let me start off by saying you are not grown. What goes on in our house, stays in our house unless it's an emergency, do you understand?" She nodded her head yes.

"And what do you think daddy is cursing for when we're in the room?"

"He says the F word and then your name after. I thought you were tickling him or playing with his feet. Daddy doesn't like people doing that." I stared to see if she were lying but the innocence in her eyes told me she wasn't. She had no idea about sex and I'm keeping it like that.

"Your ass be moaning too Jaime." I heard when we started walking back over. I had Dree go get back in the pool with Percy Jr.

"She ok?" Dreek asked and sat me on his lap.

"Yea, she thinks I play with your feet. You can't be loud when I'm riding that ride baby."

"I knew it." Jaime shouted.

"Shut the fuck up." Dreek was mad as hell Jaime kept clowning him.

"Jaime, you don't want me to tell them the sounds you make."

"Bridget, keep your mouth closed." We all started laughing.

Jaime is a damn fool and he never wanted anyone to know much about him when it came to women. The only chick we've ever met is Bridget and she ain't about to let us meet another bitch. She loves the hell out of Jaime but I hope they last. Jaime can be a jackass for sure.

"We got a problem." Robert said after looking at his phone. He passed it to Dreek and I shook my head. Evidently, when the people came to get Sabrina, she was gone.

"We'll deal with it later." Dreek handed the phone back.

"Great another bitch to worry about." I sucked my teeth and went to stand.

"A bitch, I will get. Don't you worry about nothing but how I'm going to eat the shit out your pussy tonight." He whispered in my ear.

"And I'm going to suck the skin off your dick. You're going to be cursing a lot more." I stuck my tongue in his ear and felt his dick rising under me.

"I know just what you like daddy."

"You sure do and its why you're the wife." He stuck his tongue in my mouth and everyone got up to leave.

"Y'all so corny. You know we have to make up."

"Do it later, damn." Percy said and told us they were going to the room to change. We were all meeting in the restaurant for dinner.

"Is everything done?" Dreek asked Cameron and I stared at him.

"Yea. Come on J." Cameron grabbed my hand and Dreek told me to take Dree and he was taking my son.

"Umm ok. I'll see you in a few." He kissed me and we parted ways.

****

"Where are we going? All my things are in the room." I told Cameron who made me get in her car with Dree.

"We'd rather go to a different hotel."

"Huh?" I asked and sat there texting Dreek. He told me to be quiet and not to worry. I put my phone down and looked over at Dree who had a grin on her face.

"Why are you smiling missy?"

"Nana said if I tell, it will be the first time I get a beating and she's going to make me live with Queenie." I laughed so hard, I almost choked.

"If she makes me live with her, I'm going to stab her in the eye with my favorite pencil while she sleeps."

"DREE!" I shouted.

I was surprised she spoke of stabbing someone, but then again, it's Queenie. She never had to worry about her again and I made sure of it. We pulled up at some hotel that you had to look up to see how high it went. I asked the

196

receptionist how many floors it had and she told me twenty-two.

"This is big Jiao." Dree grabbed my hand and held it tight.

"It is right." Cameron pressed the elevator and we took it up to the twentieth floor. I was scared as hell because I'm afraid of heights.

"How much did this room cost?"

"Well over a thousand a night but your man paid for it so who cares?" She shrugged and opened the door.

"What the hell?" I saw Sommer, Bridget, Carrie, Dreek's mom, a few of his aunts and Cameron's mom.

"It took you long enough." Dreek's mom said.

"She gave me a hard time about leaving."

"Come on chile." She snatched my hand and made me get in the shower. I asked no questions and stared at everyone stare at me go in the bathroom. I came out with my hair wrapped up in a towel and one on my body.

"Here. He wants you." Sommer pushed a phone in my hand.

"Damn, I tried to see you in the shower." Dreek said staring at me on facetime.

"You nasty."

"I'll be anything you want J."

"Yea." I unwrapped the towel from my hair.

"From this moment forward, don't ask any questions."

"Huh?"

"I love you Jiao and I'll see you soon." He hung the phone up. I looked around the room and everyone was staring at me. Dreek's mom came towards me with my wedding dress and I broke down crying. I knew then what was going on and I couldn't believe they kept it from me.

"Thank goodness she isn't wearing makeup yet." Susie came over and hugged me.

"When did you get here?" She wiped my face and took me in the room.

"You have to get dressed. We can discuss everything later." A woman came in and had me sit in a chair. She began blow drying my hair, while another woman came in to do my nails and feet. Once they finished, Bridget came in to do my make-up. When she was done, I had no idea who I was looking at.

"Don't you dare fucking cry and mess up my makeup." I laughed because she was as rude as Jaime. I fanned my face and it stopped my tears.

"Time to get dressed mommy." Dree said and passed me the tiara. Everyone stopped moving. Dreek's mom had tears running down her face and now so did I. This is the first time Dree has ever called me that.

"Dree, are you ok calling me mommy?"

"Yea. I asked my daddy if it was ok and he said yes because you're adopting me anyway." She asked me to bend down to put my tiara on but Carrie had her wait until we put my dress on.

"Oh my God Jiao. Dreek is going to lose his mind when he sees you." Sommer said and snapped a photo.

"You think so."

"Hell yea." They all shouted and made me laugh.

My dress was strapless like most with a six-foot train attached. It was fitted perfectly and had little diamond like ıach area. I can't really describe it but just

. beautiful and expensive gown. Cameron passed me

 Jimmy Choos I purchased to match the dress and Dree kept

asking to put the tiara on. The reason she had to wait is because

the veil is attached.

"Jiao, this is from me." Sommer handed me a diamond

tennis bracelet with x and o's on it from Tiffany's. I thanked

and hugged her.

"J, this is from me." Cameron said and passed me a

light blue hair pin. I looked at her.

"Girl shut up. I had to get something blue and it's all I

could find." She sucked her teeth. I forgot the saying,

"*Something borrowed, something blue, something old,*

*something new.*"

"This is from me J." It was Dreek's mom handing me a

diamond choker. It matched perfectly with the dress.

"This is borrowed and I want my shit back." We all

started cracking up.

"J, this is something old and it came from your mom.

She always told me to keep this just in case anything happened to her." Her and my mom were pretty tight. They didn't hang out all the time but they were close. She opened the box and it was a pair of diamond teardrop earrings that I always told her I wanted but she forbid me to wear them. I can't believe she had Susie keep them for me.

"Oh no heffa. Cry later." Bridget started fanning me with a piece of paper. A few tears fell but not a lot. She cussed me out quietly, when I cried after Dree called me mommy.

"Can I put it on now?" Dree asked and Carrie told her yes. I stood up, they put Dree on a chair and helped her put it on. She was cheesing and excited to say she helped me get dressed to marry her daddy.

*KNOCK! KNOCK!* We heard at the door and Sommer went to get it.

"Oh Lord." I heard her say.

"Come on dammit. You know I don't want to be in this suit all night." I heard Owen yelling out in the front. Everybody sucked their teeth and walked out front. I held Dree back with me to talk to her.

"Dree, you look very, very pretty."

"Thank you, mommy."

"Dree honey. I love you, you know that right?" She nodded.

"Ok. I love how you call me mommy but I want you to know, I'm not trying to make you forget your other mommy."

"I know. No one can make me forget her. She's not coming back and you're the only person I want to be my mommy now. Are you ok with me calling you mommy?" She hit me with a question.

"Of course baby. Let's get ready to marry your daddy."

"Yuk. I'm not marrying him." She ran in the other room.

I checked myself over in the mirror and smiled. I wish my mom were here and my dad could walk me down the aisle but I'm sure they're watching over me. Some may think I hate my dad and in a way, I do. I hate him for trying his hand at selling drugs for a come up and getting me and my mom in his mess but he was still my dad.

"WELL I'LL BE DAMNED. MY NEPHEW IS GOING TO FUCK THE SHIT OUT OF YOU TONIGHT?

Y'ALL STAYING IN THIS ROOM BECAUSE I DO NOT WANT TO HEAR NO SCREAMING." Owen yelled out and Dreek's mom smacked him on the back of his head.

"What I tell you about putting your damn hands on me?"

"Get your perverted ass mind out the gutter then nigga." They were going back and forth like sisters and brothers do.

"Unfortunately, he's walking you down the aisle, per Dreek. He said his other uncles are worse than Owen, so he'll take his chances with him." Susie said.

"Shitttttt. Wait til they see her. Their ass going to wish they were Dreek tonight. DAMN, YOU FINE!" All of us started laughing the entire way down on the elevator.

"Jiao, you didn't know about the wedding and we didn't know how to ask you which wedding song you wanted to walk down the aisle to, so we took a vote and agreed on one. We felt like it fit the two of you." Sommer said as we stood outside some banquet hall.

"What is it?"

"It's one a lot of people use but it's you."

"What?" I had my hand on my hip.

"The closer I get to you, by Roberta Flack."

"Ok. I'm good with it." My mom listened to those type of songs a lot so me walking down the aisle to a song with sentimental lyrics such as those, was perfect and I'm glad they picked it.

"Yoooooo. Dreek is going to bug out when he sees you." Jaime said when he came out. Him and Robert gave me a hug.

I guess they all remembered the rehearsal because everyone was partnered up. Sommer was the only one who didn't have a position but everyone knew she was the matron of honor without me saying it. She may not have been married yet, but they're next.

"You ready sexy." Owen asked and licked his lips staring at me.

"I'm ready for my man to fuck the shit out of me later. I know that." He stared at me and I winked. If he could talk shit, so could I.

# Dreek

My ass was nervous as fuck standing at the damn altar waiting on Jiao to come. I set this shit up the other day and had to pay a lot of money for it to come out right. The money didn't matter as much as the look on her face when she graced the aisle. I glanced around the church to make sure all my security was at each exit and some were meshed in with the crowd. There's no way anyone was getting in here and tearing my shit up; especially with my family in here.

The music started playing and the doors opened. The hall was so damn crowded it took me a minute to even see the beginning of the wedding party, which was my mom walking with one of my other uncles. Then Cameron and Bash. I tried to get him to be my best man too but he refused. His ass wanted to walk down the aisle with Cameron. I called him a bitch. Carrie and Robert came in, then Jaime and Bridget. Next was the flower girl and ring bearer which we all know was Dree and Percy Jr. Sommer came in last and the doors closed. Percy patted my shoulder.

"Yo, wait until you see her." Jaime whispered and I looked at him.

"She's bad bro." I wasn't mad at him for saying it but mad he got to see her first but that's how weddings go. The music started to play and the doors opened up.

*The closer I get to you, the more you make me see, by giving me all you got, your love has captured me, Over and over again, I tried to tell myself that we can never be more than friends, and all the while inside I knew, it was real, the way you make me feel.*

As the music played, everyone stood and I saw people with their phones taking photos and recording. I still had yet to see her. A few seconds later, I could see my uncle Owen grinning hard as hell and thought maybe he wasn't the right person to escort her down the aisle. I can't imagine what he was saying to her. When she came in view, I swear, I lost my breath.

"DAMN." I said and my boys heard me.

"Told you." Jaime said. My uncle stood there holding his arm in hers and waiting for the song to end. The reverend asked who was giving her away. My uncle spoke up and placed her hand in mine.

"You look beautiful Jiao." I wiped her eyes.

"I love you Dreek."

"I love you too." I cupped her face and placed a gentle kiss on her lips.

The reverend started the ceremony and asked us if we wanted to recite our vows. I asked Jiao what she wanted. It was spur of the moment and I didn't know if she had anything written.

"I'll go first." She handed her bouquet to Sommer and stared in my eyes.

"Andreek Puryear, you are by the far, the most arrogant, ignorant, rude, reckless and aggressive man I've ever met." I heard a few chicks say *you got that right.*

"But you're perfect for me. I love everything about you and no matter how much of a front you put up for everyone, I know you love me the same. It's like the song says, the closer I

207

get to you, the more I learn, the more I love, and the more I prayed we stayed together." I smiled because I felt the same.

"We've had some very trying times but through it all, you're still the only man I want. You bring me so much joy and happiness that I love waking up to you every day, even when you get on my nerves. You are the father of my children, and the love of my life. I am going to spend the rest of my life showing you, you made the right choice picking me to be your wife." She wiped the few tears from my eyes. The shit she spit was deep and again, she had me weak.

"Jiao, you are a piece of work and if anyone told me you'd be my wife, I would have told them otherwise. Matter of fact, Percy predicted this right here and I disagreed but he was right." I pointed to us.

"J, in all my life, I never pictured myself standing here with you or any woman, but you stole my heart and it wasn't a damn thing I could do about it. I tried to be mean and hurtful to you and nothing worked because the heart wants, what it wants and that was you." She was crying hard. I handed her my handkerchief and lifted her face.

"You know I would do anything just to see a smile on your face and there ain't nothing I won't do for you. Jiao, I don't want you to ever doubt my love for you." She smiled.

"Who knew I could love someone else besides my daughter, my mom and now my son? I'm a special kind of dude and I know it's not easy loving me. I want to thank you for sticking around and making me love you."

"Dreek."

"I'm here to say I'm giving you my time, my money, my heart and anything else you want to make sure I'm yours. I don't want anyone but you baby." I took the handkerchief and finished wiping the tears falling down her face. I looked up and all her damn bridesmaids were crying and so was my mom, Sommer's mom, my aunts and a few other ladies. My speech was the shit though.

"Well, that was quite a vow." The reverend said and finished the ceremony.

"You may kiss the bride." I pulled her close, her arms went around my neck and we kissed. This time it wasn't nasty like we usually do because of the kids and old people here.

"Everyone stand and help me introduce Mr. and Mrs. Andreek Puryear." We jumped the broom thing and started walking out. People were clapping and recording. Once we got outside, we made a right to go take pictures before we went into the other ballroom where the reception was. The rest of the wedding party came in and we cut up with the photos.

"How you feel being Mrs. Andreek Puryear?" I stopped her from walking out the room where the pictures were. We had to wait for the DJ to introduce us.

"I feel like you're going to be a daddy again in about seven months." I rubbed her stomach.

"Damn Jiao. You were definitely placed in my life for a reason. I love you."

"What to have your kids?" I laughed.

"That and to calm me down. You love our kids, take care of home and still ready to kill for me."

"You better believe it."

"Introducing Mr. and Mrs. Puryear." We heard the DJ yell and ran out and into the room. After speaking to everyone the DJ called us to the dance floor for our first dance. Jiao said she didn't give him a song to play but it didn't matter. The one I had him play was good enough. I reached my hand out for her and kissed the top of it like she was a queen, well she's mine that's for sure.

*There's something that I want to say, but words sometimes get in the way, I just want to show my feelings for you*

You are my lady, played by Freddie Jackson. She and I were so close that I sung some of the words in her ear and she started crying again. I kissed her tears away and continued dancing until the song went off. People started clapping and she walked over to the DJ and had him play a song. I didn't know what it was at first.

"Oooh this is my shit." I heard my mom yell out, which means it's an older song.

*Share my life, take me for what I am, Cause I'll never change, all my colors for you, take my love, I'll never ask for too much, just all that you are and everything you do.*

I have nothing by Whitney Houston, played in the background. When she starting singing the words to me, I had to move back. I had no idea she had a voice like that. She even started hitting the high notes. The DJ turned the music down a little and she kept going. Everyone stopped talking and stared at her. Shit, I was in awe myself and had to smile. I was impressed and knew all the bitches would be jealous. Everyone clapped and my mom ran up and said she want Jiao singing at her next birthday party and they were going out for karaoke, so she could win her some money.

"Damn baby, I had no idea you could blow." She raised an eyebrow.

"You know I can blow." I laughed at her nasty ass.

"I love your voice mommy." Dree came over.

"Thanks baby. I think it's time for your dance with daddy. You ready." She shook her head yes.

I didn't know what she was talking about but they played the Luther dance with my father song. I saw her sit down and could tell she was upset about her dad. I nodded to my uncle and had him go get her and offer a dance. She turned him down but when Percy Jr. went to her, she stood up and wiped her face.

"Damn Jiao. What that little nigga got that I don't?" My uncle yelled out. She stuck her tongue out at him.

"Thank you, baby." She kissed me.

"Anything for you J." The two of us danced until the song finished and sat down to eat. The reverend blessed the table and the waiters began bringing the food out. Percy and Bash gave a best man speech where they clowned me for Jiao locking me down. Sommer stood and gave her toast and made Jiao cry talking about her mom. It was very emotional for her. I ended up having to take her out to calm down. Dree came running behind me and wiped her eyes.

"I love both of you very much." She kissed Dree and sent her inside.

"Dreek, thank you for everything. The wedding, the dance and loving me."

"Jiao, I know you think I'm a bastard at times but know you and the kids are always my main concern. We are one baby and when you hurt so do I." I kissed her and we walked in the reception while everyone danced to the damn cupid shuffle. I swear, this is the black people's anthem at weddings. She stayed on the dance floor and I went to sit down.

"A married man." Percy gave me a hug and sat next to me.

"I know, you called it."

"I sure did."

"She looks happy bro." I stared at her on the dance floor and she was smiling and dancing with everyone.

"She does, right? I hope I can keep her that way."

"Bro, she ain't leaving your ass. I hate to say it but you're stuck with her. She's as crazy as you and you should be happy she let you put a ring on it."

"I am." The song went off and the Cha Cha slide came on. I noticed Jiao trying to come off the dance floor and Dree

214

asking her to stay on. She held her hand and did the dance with her. She damn sure hauled ass afterwards though.

"Baby, my feet hurt."

"Why didn't you take your shoes off?" I lifted her feet on my lap and started massaging them.

"Because people were taking pictures. I couldn't have my photos without my shoes on."

"You're a mess, you know that?"

"Yup but I'm your mess now." I leaned over and kissed her.

"Hell yea you are."

"I'm ready for you to eat the shit out of my pussy." I grabbed her hand and took her out the hall and into the bathroom.

"Not here baby."

"Nah, we about to get it in." I lifted her up on the couch thing in the bathroom and went to pull her panties down, when the toilet flushed.

"Oh shit." I picked her up, threw her over my shoulder and ran out the bathroom.

"That's what you get. Let's tell everyone goodnight."
She went ahead of me inside.

"She lucky as hell to have a man like you." Some chick
said coming out the bathroom.

"Nah, I'm the lucky one." She smiled and walked off.
The DJ told everyone we were leaving and Jiao was sitting in
the chair holding lil Dreek.

"Baby, he feels hot. We need to take him to the
hospital."

"Hold on. I don't have my car here. Let me get
Jaime's."

"Dree, go get your shoes on." I heard Jiao say. By the
time we found someone's car to use and leave it was after
midnight.

We walked in the emergency room in our wedding
clothes. People stared at us but I didn't give a fuck. They
triaged my son and took him in the back right away. His fever
was extremely high.

We sat there for two hours as they took blood and
checked him over. Come to find out he had an ear infection

and more teeth coming in. The doctor told us it was normal and gave him an antibiotic. We could've left but he wanted to make sure the fever started to break first. Once it did, he handed us the prescription and sent us on our way.

"Is he ok?" Sommer and my mom came running in as we were walking out.

"Yea." I explained what the doctor said and they left when we did.

"I'm going to wash him up and lay him down." Jiao said and had Dree go with her.

I locked up and started taking my clothes off. We had to postpone the honeymoon at the last minute because Jiao didn't want to leave my son and frankly, I didn't feel comfortable leaving him either. I had my wife beater and pants on and went to check on her. It was funny watching her get the kids ready for bed in her wedding dress.

"Go check on Dree baby. I'll get him finished."

"You sure."

"I'm sure. You do so much already."

"It's because I love my family." She kissed me and stepped out.

I finished changing my son and gave him a bottle with some clear shit in it. Jiao said it was Pedialyte. Some shit to keep him hydrated since he didn't want milk. Once he finished, I cleaned him up and laid in his room with him on my chest until he fell asleep.

"Come on baby." I opened my eyes and lil Dreek was no longer on my chest and Jiao was in her pajamas.

"Shit, I'm sorry babe."

"Dreek, its fine. We're married now and I know it was an exhausting day. I just want to lay in your arms tonight." I followed her in the room and took a quick shower to give her what she wanted. I hopped in the bed naked and she fell asleep as soon as her head hit my chest. If this is what it's like to be married, I can definitely get used to this.

# Sommer

I have to say, I'm happy Jiao allowed me to be a part of her wedding. We've done everything together growing up and it would've felt crazy not to have been there. It made me want to marry Percy sooner but I kept refusing. He never told me what happened to Kevin but I figured it out because I haven't seen him around and the checks haven't been cashed. Usually he'd run to the bank and deposit them quick.

The only person standing in my way was Charlotte and it's because I didn't want her finding out and ruining my day. I saw the amount of security Dreek had in place when he married J and I didn't want that. Of course, I don't want anything to happen but I also want to be carefree.

Today, Percy wanted me to come over to the restaurant and start adding things to the menu. I really didn't care about working there and he knew it. However, he told me to get a feel of it. I dropped Percy Jr. off at school and my daughter was with Percy's parents as always. They had to take turns with my mom and dad though. Percy Jr. always wanted to be under us for some reason.

"Good morning boss." Carol said when I stepped in the restaurant. It was a little after ten when I arrived. People were cleaning and setting up for the afternoon rush. Percy told me the place has been crowded ever since the grand opening and the money was right.

"Good morning. How are you?" I smiled and she came behind me to the office. I opened the door and covered my mouth. There were vases full of lilies all over my office. I turned around and she handed me an envelope.

*Sommer,*

*I know you're hesitant about getting married with a certain person lurking outside but today is your day, whether you're ready or not. I'm not waiting another day for you to be my wife. Your hair appointment is at 10:15 so get to it.* I looked at Carol and she shrugged her shoulders. I picked my phone up and called Jiao.

"Hurry up bitch. I don't want to be in the hairdresser all day." Is how she answered the phone.

"You knew?"

"Duh. Who you think told him lilies were your favorite? Now hurry up." I hopped in my car, drove to the salon and everyone was there; including Susie and Percy's mom. Here I was thinking they were still focused on Jiao's wedding and the entire time they were helping Percy.

"It's about time y'all getting married. Shit, you were engaged before Dreek and I."

"Well yo ass wanted a speed wedding." Dreek's mom said and we all laughed.

"Whatever. He needed to be my husband before putting all his kids in me. Speaking of kids, have you told Percy you're pregnant again." J asked and everyone stared at me.

"What? Shit, I thought you told everyone." She shrugged and sat under the chair.

I found out about my pregnancy two weeks ago but with the shit Kevin did and Charlotte out there, I didn't want to alert Percy and make him more paranoid then he already is. Bad enough, he has someone following me too.

"Damn, they just knocking y'all ass up." Cameron came in talking shit with her pregnant ass. She was going on six months and Bash had her take a leave of absence. He was worried about her falling or as he says, getting some disease from the nasty ass hospital. He is just as extra as Dreek and Percy.

"Anyway, I'm going to tell him tonight."

"You better because you know Dreek's mom can't hold water." I rolled my eyes and she popped Jiao on the head. The door opened and in walked some bitch who appeared to be familiar. She stared straight at Jiao and I knew then who she was; we all did.

"What the fuck you looking at Sabrina?" She rolled her eyes and sat in one of the chairs. I knew the pettiness was about to start when she picked the phone up and placed it on speaker. All of us turned to look at her when Dreek said hello.

"Hey baby."

"Where you at Sabrina?" He didn't respond to her calling him that, but it was odd that he didn't hang up.

"At the nail salon getting ready for our date later."

"Oh yea. I'll hit you up where to meet me."

"Ok love." She hung up and stared at Jiao who had a water bottle in her hand with a smile on her face.

"I'm about to drag this bitch." Bridget put her hair up.

"It's all good Bridget. She can have Dreek if she wants. I mean now that we're married, he can have a mistress because it's all she'll ever be."

"Bitch, he ain't marry you." Sabrina stood up and so did all of us. Percy's mom pulled me behind her.

"Oh no. Let's see." Jiao picked her phone up.

"Hey baby. I miss you." J said when Dreek answered.

"Well get home and make love to your husband. Shit, you been out all day. I need some of that good stuff."

"And I need that good dick. I'll be home in a few. I love you."

"I love you too. And J." He called out before she hung up.

"Yea babe."

"Tell Sabrina the shit she trying to pull ain't going to work. Us meeting up, you already know about, so she playing herself." Jiao smirked and Sabrina stormed out the salon.

"Bitchhhhhhhhh. That's what the fuck I'm talking about." Carrie yelled out.

"I'm sorry Sommer. Today is your day and she came in here trying to ruin it. I know all about him meeting her. She's been calling him everyday and he kept ignoring her. He offered to get his number changed but I told him no. She didn't deserve the satisfaction."

"You ok with him meeting her?"

"I trust him to do what he needs, to get whatever information he has to from her. He also knows if he fucks up in any way, I'll fuck him up and leave his ass."

"Yea ok. You ain't going nowhere."

"You know that's exactly what he said." J had us in there cracking up.

I sat down in the chair and let the lady start on my hair. The entire time we were in there, all of us cracked jokes and carried on about the bullshit with Hector. Jiao, explained as much as she could without saying too much. We weren't sure who knew who and didn't want to take the chance on someone running back with the information.

After we were done, all of them came to my house and I got another surprise when the nanny opened the door for me. My dress was laid out on the couch and there were shoes, accessories and so much other shit. I don't know when Percy picked all this stuff out but I appreciated him for doing it.

Susie came in and handed me something in a white box. I opened it up and started crying. It was her veil when she married my father. I've often told her, I wanted to wear it at my own wedding and I guess she remembered.

"Stop crying before Bridget comes in here and fights both of us. You know how she gets once she does your makeup." She dabbed the handkerchief on my eyes.

"I know. Thank you so much ma."

"Ma. That bitch didn't birth you." I turned around and saw Charlotte coming in the front door. I also saw Jiao and everyone else come running down the steps. How the fuck did she get here and who let her in?

"I knew you would come around." I stood up and walked over to her.

"Why wouldn't I come to my daughter's wedding?" I didn't have time for the games she was playing. I knew just like everyone else, that she wanted something.

"To make your father pay for leaving me. Now where is the paperwork and USB?" She pulled a pocket knife out and I laughed at her. What in the hell was she going to do with that little shit?

"Percy destroyed it. You happy now? There's no need for you to come around any longer."

"Oh, but there is. You have a brother out there and until you give me what you have, I'm not going to tell you who he is."

"I already know who he is. Matter of fact, he's walking me down the aisle with my father." Her mouth dropped to the floor.

"Ok. Ok. Sommer look. I'm sorry for not being a better mom. Do you think we can make up?"

"Hell no. Are you fucking crazy?" Susie answered for me and it infuriated Charlotte. She charged Susie.

*POW! POW!* Charlotte's body dropped. Her eyes were opened and blood leaked from her head and chest.

"I'm sorry Sommer." Susie said and looked at me.

"Don't be. She had it coming." I hugged her and asked Bridget to call Jaime and let him know what went down, and that everything was still going to happen. Of course, Percy called and flipped the fuck out over Charlotte coming here. I had to calm him down because he wanted to come here.

"Alright bitch. Let me fix your make up and don't fucking mess it up again." I had to laugh at her because like Jiao said, her and Jaime are a trip. And no, Tina J is not doing a spin off on them or Sommer's parents.

**** 

"How does it feel to be married to the best-looking man in the world?" Percy asked on the way to the reception.

"I don't know because I have the best-looking man in the universe." He pecked my lips and pulled me on top of him in the limo.

"Got damn Sommer. You wet as fuck." He moaned out when I slid down. The reception spot wasn't far at all and we both wanted to get it in before we got there.

"Always for you. Mmmmm Percy, it feels so good." I rocked back and forth and watched him bite down on his lip. He squeezed my ass like he always did and lifted me up, just to have me drop harder on his dick. I never understood why men wanted a woman to do that.

"We're here baby. Cum with me." His hand was on my pearl and we fucked the hell out of each other.

"I love you baby." He kissed my neck as he came and both of us sat there trying to catch our breath.

"I love you too Percy." He reached in one of the cabinets and passed me some tissues to clean up. I told him we needed to go in the bathroom before we entered the party. Fortunately, we went in and ended up sexing each other in there too. Jiao came banging on the door and told us to save it for later.

"After you Mr. Miller." I opened the door.

"Nah. After you Mrs. Miller." He stood behind me and held it open. We walked in the reception hand in hand as the happiest couple on earth. I wouldn't change anything when it comes to my life. I was happy and Percy was going to make sure I stayed this way.

# Dreek

"This is a toast to the married men in the room."
Sommer's dad lifted his glass and so did the rest of us. We
were at her parents' house chilling. There was no specific
reason besides him and Sommer just returning from their
honeymoon.

"Percy, I want to thank you for loving my daughter and
making her a better woman." He nodded.

"Don't get me wrong, my wife has done a hell of a job
raising her but before you, that punk ass nigga took her through
a lot and I didn't think she would allow another man in her life.
Now look, you gave her my granddaughter, grandson and
another one on the way." He claimed Percy Jr. as his own and
Susie dared anyone tell her she wasn't his grandmother.

We all knew she couldn't have kids but she damn sure
had Sommer and Percy's kids all the time. Sommer's dad
finally broke down and said they could adopt if she wanted but
Susie turned the offer down. She said she was too old now and
her grandkids were enough.

"Andreek, I don't know how Jiao did it but I'm glad she did." Everyone started laughing.

"I'm serious. As we all know, a bitch as he calls them, couldn't even get Dreek to say he missed her. Jiao came in his life and she had him missing, needing and loving her." I sucked my teeth.

"Anyway, her mom would have loved you for her. She always said Jiao would have to find a man as evil and crazy as her. She has definitely found the right person."

"My wife is not evil or crazy."

"Sheittttttt." All of them said at once.

"Y'all know I'm telling her right."

"Whatever." We all took a drink.

"Anyway, how are we handling Hector?" Percy asked.

"I say we get a crew ready and go over there. He won't be expecting us and right now is the perfect time to hit. He's still trying to rebuild his shitty fields, so us entering Cuba is most likely, not on his mind."

"Sounds good to me Dreek. Let's set up a meeting tomorrow with the team and go from there." Percy stood and poured another drink.

For the remainder of the night, all we did was get fucked up. I had to call Jiao to pick me up and everyone else ended up doing the same with their women. I made J pull over twice for me to throw up. I'm a drinker but tonight I think my ass over did it. We were mixing drinks and getting high. It felt good not to have someone scheming on us as we enjoyed ourselves.

When I got home, Jiao helped me in the house and told me to lay on the couch. She wasn't cleaning up any vomit and wanted to get a good night's sleep. I ignored her, followed her upstairs, stripped and laid right next to her. For someone who didn't want me in the bed with her, she damn sure was snuggled under me.

****

"Valdez, is everything set up for our arrival next week?" I asked him on the speakerphone. We were having the meeting to get Hector, in the conference room of the warehouse. I was tired as hell but this needed to be handled and then I'd go home and sleep.

"Yea. The only people informed of you coming is my cousin and that's because he'll be the one filling me in on Hector's whereabouts. I have a few people at the airport so when you arrive the video footage will be switched to the previous hour. Therefore, no one will notice you step off the plane."

"Perfect." I said a few more words to him and disconnected the call. Percy and I excused everyone and walked to my office.

"Mr. Puryear, we have an unidentified vehicle on the property. My secretary stated in the intercom. I pulled up the camera and laughed.

"Make sure your door closed when she gets here. I damn sure don't want to hear you and sis getting it in." Percy laughed.

"Nigga, don't think I don't know Sommer's ass wasn't in here the other day doing the same thing."

"Whatever."

"Send her up." I told my secretary and watched Jiao look around. This is her first time coming here, besides the night I found out about Hector.

"Mr. Puryear." I glanced up and Barbara was standing there. This woman was pretty and had a body to die for. However, women were off limits to all of us. Percy and I didn't play that office romance shit. It caused too many problems and its shit we don't need.

"What can I help you with?" She came over to my desk and leaned over to hand me some paper. Her breasts almost came out her shirt and the skirt was way above the knee, which is not what the dress code required. It doesn't take a genius to know shorty wanted me and has, for quite some time. She flirted with me a lot and I always ignored her. It seems that once I married Jiao, her advances become more aggressive.

"These papers came in yesterday and require your signature." I leaned back in my chair and stared at her. She bit down on her lip in an erotic way and I had to smile. Not because I wanted her but the desperation to fuck me was evident.

234

"Barbara, let me ask you a question."

"Yes." She sat on my desk and crossed her legs.

I looked back at my computer and noticed security allowing Jiao access inside and she had a bag in her hand, which means I only had a few minutes to get this woman out my office. I'm not doing anything but Jiao is extremely jealous and this doesn't look good.

"You wanna fuck me?" She smirked and uncrossed her legs.

"Mr. Puryear, I know how you feel about office romance." She hopped off the desk and stood in front of me.

"However, yes I would love to have an affair with you." I nodded my head.

"I appreciate your honesty and you're fired."

"What?"

"Melissa, send T.M. up here for a removal."

"Right away sir." T.M. is the female who worked for us. She was the manager of our warehouse and she gave zero fucks about anything.

"Mr. Puryear. Why are you firing me? You know the feeling is mutual. I've seen the way you watch me walk by." She had her hand on my chest. I snatched her wrist and snapped it.

"You are disrespectful as fuck yo. You know my stand on employees fucking, you also know I'm married and you're still trying. I can't stand a desperate bitch."

"Oh my God. Its broken."

"Mr. Puryear, look who I found." T.M. came in with a smile on her face and it changed when she saw Barbara on the floor crying.

"Hey babe. I brought you lunch. Ugh, what happened?" I ran my hand through her hair and had her face me. I let my tongue meet hers and stopped because my dick was swelling up.

"She tried to fuck me." I said and took my lunch from her.

"Word!" T.M. said and grabbed Barbara's hair.

"You know what to do." She nodded and drug her out the room kicking and screaming.

"Let me find out."

"You won't find out shit. Percy and I don't play that employee love shit. Do you know she wanted to be my mistress?"

"Did you tell her the position is filled by your wife, along with the rest of them?"

"Nah, because my wife has been holding out. I may need to get a mistress to handle this." I grabbed my dick and she ran behind me and wrapped her arms around my neck. You would think she had me in the choke hold but her strength wasn't anywhere near mine. I grabbed her arm and pulled her around to sit on my lap.

"Eat some of this." I put a French fry in her mouth.

"How you know I didn't eat yet?"

"Even if you did, I know my baby has you hungry again."

"You calling me fat?" She took another fry and fed it to me.

"Never babe. But that pussy is a different story.

"Oh yea." She stood up and took her shirt off.

237

"Yo, hold up J." I lifted her up and ran to lock my office door. There's no way anyone would get a free peek at my wife.

"Damn J." She had removed all of her clothes by the time I turned around.

"What were you saying about my pussy being fat?" She lifted her leg on my desk and started playing with her pussy. I unbuckled my jeans and let them and my boxers hit the floor.

"I think you forgot what I told you about this pussy being mine." She let her head fall back as she laughed. I kissed her neck and laid her on my desk. I didn't care what fell of my desk and broke because it could be replaced.

"You feel so got damn good J." She had her hands cupping my face and pulled me in for a kiss.

"I swear every time you make love to me, I fall more in love with you." I stopped and stared in her eyes.

"I feel the same Jiao Puryear." She smiled and wrapped her legs around m my back.

"Mr. Puryear, T.M. wanted you to know the situation is handled." My secretary said and I ignored her to finish with J.

238

When we finished, I had her go in my bathroom and clean herself up. She came out looking as beautiful as she did going in. Jiao, definitely had a hold on me. I don't know or care how she got me this way but I like it.

"I'll see you tomorrow Mr. Puryear. Nice meeting you Mrs. Puryear." Melissa said on our way out and Jiao smiled.

"Will I see you at home later Mr. Puryear?"

"I'm coming home now to spend time with my wife and kids."

"I'll see you soon babe." She got in her truck and I followed suit. This married life ain't so bad after all.

# Jiao

Sommer's wedding was perfect for her and I'm happy her and Percy decided to do it now. Dreek and I have been married for almost a month and we were going on our honeymoon. Neither of us was comfortable leaving the kids after our wedding so we held off for a while. However, today was going to be the last one, dealing with the bullshit and I couldn't wait for it to be over.

"Get your fucking hands off me! I shouted to the dude Ernesto." I was in the bathroom of the movies washing my hands when he came in and yanked me out. Dreek and I left the kids with his mom so we could have a date night with the crew.

"You have a smart-ass mouth for a bitch who's going to die." He was smiling and I could see lust written on his face too.

"Bitch!" I put my hands on my hips.

As bad as I wanted to hook off, I couldn't. I had to keep in mind that my child depended on me to keep him or her safe in my stomach. No one knew about the pregnancy yet, except Dreek and I, and it's better to keep it this way. We knew the time would come when Hector came for me and that time is now.

"Yea bitch. Hector should have let me kill you a long time ago."

"Too bad he didn't." I rolled my eyes and let him drag me to the black SUV. I know everyone believes I'm in the bathroom but I pray Dreek realizes it before this punk gets me too far for him to save me.

"I have her." He spoke in the phone on Bluetooth to Hector, who chuckled when Ernesto told him.

"I'm sure she gave you a run for your money."

"Not this time boss. The gun in her face kept her quiet."

"Hola, Jiao. Long time no hear from."

"What the fuck you want Hector?"

"First off, you still owe me some of that pussy." I laughed. This nigga stalking my shit.

"Keep going."

"You're going to hand over all of your father's businesses to me and whatever debt he had, you're going to pay."

"That's where you have me fucked up. I'm not him and you don't scare me. As far as the businesses, you're too late. They're all sold and I received a great deal of money for them." I heard him laugh like it was funny.

"And this pussy belongs to one man and one man only. I dare you to touch it." I toyed with him because he hated my husband and any mention of Dreek, pissed him off.

"FUCK HIM!" He yelled out and I laughed harder.

"Awww, don't tell me your upset hearing my husband's name."

"Husband?" He questioned. I guess now that Mandy's ass is dead, he didn't have his so-called informant to relay the information.

"Yes, my husband. The wedding was beautiful. Your invitation must've gotten lost in the mail." I was fucking with him now.

"He'll be a grieving husband soon because your ass will die by my hands. Let me hear you laugh now?" I remained quiet. Ernesto finished speaking with him and hung the phone up.

Bzzzzz. Bzzzzz my phone began to vibrate. I forgot it was in my clutch. I glanced down at it and saw Dreek asking where I was.

**Me:** *It's time*

**My love:** *No doubt. You good.*

243

**Me:** *Yup as long as you got me.*

**My Love:** *There's never a time I won't. Keep my daughter safe.* I smiled because we had one of each but he wanted a daughter with me.

**Me:** *I will but hurry.*

**My love:** *Already in route. Love you*

I sent him back a text with the kissy face emoji and placed the phone in my clutch. I leaned on the door and closed my eyes. If he was taking me to the address where the tracker had the trucks at, it's going to be a long ride.

****

I woke up, out the truck and in a bed with only my panties and bra on. How did I not feel anyone take me out? I was tired but damn. Looking around the room, I'm assuming it's the house Hector stays in when he's here. It was beautiful and you could tell a woman decorated it.

244

I moved the covers off and stood up. The floor had a plush rug and felt good under my feet. I walked over to the window and noticed a few guards standing outside smoking and talking. One looked up and had a huge grin on his face. I remembered my clothes weren't on and backed away.

"Still have a body to die for." Hector said as he leaned on the door. Hector was a very handsome man and had he done me right, we may have been together.

"Yup and it would've been yours, if you had kept your dick to yourself." He came towards me.

"If you wouldn't have been a virgin and gave it to me sooner, we'd still be together." I tossed my head back laughing.

"Hector, who are you kidding. The only reason I'm here is for you to attempt to get the pussy and.-"

"No attempt. I'm going to get it and you're going to make sure it's worth it. Otherwise I can kill you now and get it over with." I never responded because my heart was beating fast and praying Dreek would make it to me.

"Strip."

He said and licked his lips. I barely had clothes on and he wanted me to remove the rest. I stood there until he took the gun out his waist and pointed it at my stomach. I tried to hold the tears in but I couldn't.

"Oh, you thought I didn't know." He smirked.

"Funny thing Jiao. When you fall asleep, make sure you close your messages and lock your phone."

"So, you know Dreek's coming?"

"He'll never find you here." I had to smile to myself because if he only knew.

"Hector." I tried to engage him in more conversation to stall but he wasn't falling for it.

"Strip Jiao or I swear both of you will die right now."

"You want to force me to sleep with you knowing I'm pregnant with another man's child?"

"It ain't my kid and I'll make sure to fuck you hard, so the bastard can feel my dick on its head." He came closer and I backed up. I felt the tip of the gun lift my bra strap up. I allowed it to fall off my shoulder and did the same with the other side. I reached behind, unclasped my bra and it hit the ground. Hector took his shirt off.

"Damn J. The baby has you filling out more and more. It's a shame you're going to die after I sample it." He kept taunting me.

"Now your panties. I can't wait to see her." I slowly did what he asked and they were at my ankles when the door was kicked in.

"Oh shit." I heard and bullets started flying around my head. Someone jumped on top of me and right then, I knew it was my husband.

"You good." He asked after all the shooting in the room stopped.

"Yes. He was about to.-" I started crying.

"I know. Let me get something for you to put on." He snatched the sheet off the bed and when we got off the floor, Jaime, Robert and Percy were standing there with sad faces.

"We got here in time. Jaime take her out the way we came in. It's time to kill this motherfucker." I've seen him mad a lot but this Dreek is different. He had murder on his mind and no one could stop him.

"Please don't let anything happen to him." I cried to Jaime as he put me in a truck and told the driver to take me home.

"Damn J. What about us? We came with him." Jaime always made jokes.

"Be safe and bring my husband home." I kissed his cheek and closed the door.

On the drive home, I was a nervous wreck. Not only did Hector almost rape me but I was in the back seat in just a sheet. I asked the driver if I could use his phone and he passed it to me without so much as looking in the rearview mirror. Dreek had his workers trained. I dialed my man's number and waited for him to answer.

"You better not be calling to say something happened to my wife." He answered angrily. I smiled because he was always looking out for me.

"Baby."

"What's wrong J?" I could hear panic in his voice.

"Northing babe. I wanted to make sure you're ok."

"I'm good. What about you?"

"I'm fine. Thank you."

"Don't thank me for protecting you Jiao. It's my job."

"I love you so much Dreek." I started crying.

"J, please don't cry. I won't be able to focus knowing you need me."

"Ok. I'm good." I wiped my eyes.

"Do you want me to come get you?"

"No. Get him and make sure you don't die." He started laughing.

"I love you J."

"I love you too and I'll see you soon."

"You sure will. Now go home and relax."

"I am." He hung up and I handed the phone back to the driver. I said a quick prayer to God to watch over my husband and everyone with him.

# Dreek

When I realized Jiao never returned from the bathroom, we sent the girls home and hopped on the road. I hated the fact, Jiao never had a problem handling shit on her own. Yea, it's a good thing in a way because if I can't get to her, she'll know what to do until I can. I can be mad all I want about my wife letting Hector feel her for a few seconds but at this moment, I understood why she did it.

In the beginning, I was hurt she allowed him to touch her but it was for a bigger purpose. J should have gone about it a different way but when you're in a situation, I guess you have to improvise. On the flip side, she's still a woman and unless she had a gun on her, a man can still get the upper hand. I'm happy this shit is almost over because it's long overdue, which is why I'm happy J put those tracking devices in his truck.

The place he was at, took a while for us to get to. However, we've been here a few times staking the place out when Hector was in Cuba. I needed to know as much as possible about the place because we knew it's where he'd take Jiao.

There were guards outside the spot smoking and a few walking around the perimeter. It still wasn't enough for the amount of people we had behind us. On the way here, I made calls to some of the workers and they immediately shut down shop and hopped in their cars to get here.

Each one of us went in different directions and I gave specific instructions on how to deal with Hector if they found him first. Lucky for me, I kicked the door down to where he held Jiao. My wife stood there naked and he only had a wife beater and pants on. All I saw was red.

Granted, bullets started flying, so I jumped on J to make sure she didn't get hit. She was crying and told me he almost touched her and the beast in me began to surface and J saw it.

I snatched the sheet off the bed and made sure she was fully covered before allowing Jaime to walk her downstairs.

Once the driver pulled off with her, we searched the house, top to bottom. We looked for secret walls and he was nowhere to be found. I called Valdez and asked where Hector was. He was shocked Hector was here because his cousin never told him, which made me think maybe the cousin isn't helping out after all.

He hung up and called me back two minutes later and said his cousin claimed they were in route to the airport. The reason he didn't tell Valdez about their trip here is because he wasn't with him. Evidently, Hector left in the middle of the night with his bodyguard. He didn't know where the others came from.

"Call our people at the airport and make sure the jet he came in on, doesn't pull off until we get there." I told Percy but he was already on the phone. That's the shit I'm talking about. We were in sync with one another and never had to tell the other what to do, because it was already being done.

"The tracker says they stopped at some store." Robert said and showed us on the phone.

"A store."

"Yup. Walmart to be exact."

"WALMART!" All of us shouted.

"Oh shit. You can buy weapons from Walmart now." Jaime told us.

"You think that's what they're buying?" I shrugged my shoulders.

"What the fuck is this world coming too?" I asked.

"What you mean?"

"It's a sad day when you can purchase guns to kill people in the same store you buy groceries." They all shook their heads.

"It's bad enough you can buy clothes in there." Jaime had us laughing.

"I'm serious. You ever go in there and see people with clothes and food in the same cart? The shit looks fucking crazy."

"Yooo, this nigga is shot the fuck out." Robert was cracking up in the back seat.

"How far is Walmart from here?"

"The GPS says two minutes." I drove straight there.

"You thinking what I'm thinking?" Percy asked and looked at me.

"You already know."

I parked a few cars down from where the truck was Hector came in. All the guys with me, scattered throughout the parking lot. We didn't know how many guys came with him and wanted to make sure we were covered. Women and children came in and out the store and still no Hector. At first, I thought maybe he left the truck but changed my mind when him and I'm assuming his bodyguard came out. A few seconds later, a few more guys came out and walked towards other cars. I stepped out the truck and walked over to him. I didn't care who he was or where we were at.

"What up Hector?" I hopped in the backseat and scared the shit out of him.

"So, you're going to kill me in a Walmart parking lot?"

"Yup."

PHEW! PHEW! I shot him in the head and stepped out the truck. Him and his bodyguard were good as gone.

"Is it done?"

"Yup. Let's roll." We pulled out the lot and bullets began flying. The back window came crashing down and the people who came with Hector began following us. I could have stopped but what for? My people ran them off the road, shot the cars up and pulled off.

I know people wanted me to make Hector die a slow death but prolonging it in my eyes, only wasted time and my wife needed me. Trust me, I wanted to torture the shit out of him, but I'm not about to go any longer without making sure she's ok. I dropped the guys off and made my way home. I parked, went in, locked the door and walked up the steps to find my wife.

"I'm glad you made it home to me." She smiled. I took my clothes off and sat in the tub behind her. She laid her head on my chest and mine rested on the back of the wall.

"I hope you killed him right away."

"I did like you asked." Jiao and I had a conversation previously about killing Hector and she is the one who asked me not to torture him. She felt like he didn't waste time taking her mom's life so she wanted him to face the same fate.

Sometimes avenging someone's death isn't always about torture then it is, getting it over with and moving on. It won't bring our loved ones back but at least the person is dealt with in a timely manner.

Sabrina on the other hand, met her fate the night I met her, when she tried to be funny at the salon. She claimed to have information about Hector, when in actuality all she wanted was to fuck. I would never cheat on Jiao and even though Sabrina stripped in front of me, she wasn't worth losing my wife.

"You know I'm going on birth control after this one." She turned around and sat on top of me.

"I wish you would." She sucked her teeth.

"Dreek, just give me a year to enjoy the kids. Pleaseeeeeee." She began kissing on my neck and getting me aroused.

"One year Jiao and that's it." She stood up just enough to insert my dick inside her.

"Damn baby." I let her handle me the way she wanted.

"I want my side chick to show me what I'm missing?" I said and she smirked.

"You want me to be bad for you?" We stepped out the tub.

"Always, but you do know that when you're bad, I'm badder." I told her and let her roll play my side chick and end off as my freak.

"I love you Jiao Puryear." I kissed her forehead as she laid under me.

"I love you too Andreek Puryear."

# THE END!!!!

# COMING SOON!!!

# Her Man, His

# Savage

**Tina J**

# Prologue

*That girl is a real crowd pleaser*

*Small world, all her friends know of me,*

*Young bull living like and old geaser,*

*Quick release the cash, watch it fall slowly*

The song played throughout my basement where I had a few of my boys here along with some women who came home from the club with us. I loved me some strippers and the ones in front of us dancing, were fine as hell. Their ass was huge, breasts were perky and the way they danced on the pole, had my dick harder than a chemistry test.

It was three of them but one in particular stood out from the rest. She was dark skinned and you could see how nervous she was. I thought about asking her if she was ok, but if her ass came home with us, she had to be.

Over the next ten minutes, the women danced a few more songs and were in their birthday suits by now. Each of my boys grabbed a female and disappeared into one of the rooms. This house was where we entertained bitches but I say it's mine because it's in my name.

Me and the dark-skinned chick were the ones left down here but for some reason, my dick didn't want her because something was off. If I felt like this, I always went with my gut. I excused myself from her and said I'd be right back. I picked my phone up and sent a message.

**Me**: *This bitch is suspect, you know what to do."* I put it back in my pocket and went upstairs.

"She gotta go." I told my boy Champ when I busted in the room. He was getting head by one of them. He saw my face and stood up grabbing his piece. He kicked the chick in the stomach, with no questions asked and followed me. If some shit was off we never said much and if one of us bust in on the other, it was an automatic to get rid of anyone involved.

"Where's Misfit?" He asked and we both ran to the room and kicked the door open. Shorty was letting him fuck her from the back.

"We gotta roll."

"Word. It's like that?" I nodded and he pulled out. Not even five seconds later, he shot the chick in the head. Misfit is a monster and his name fit his profile. You'll hear more about the crazy nigga later.

We ran down to the first floor and straight into at least ten motherfuckers pointing weapons at us. The chick from the basement came up fully dressed with a grin on her face. She walked over to some guy and they began slobbing one another down.

I heard screaming, which let me know the other stripper saw what Misfit did. She came running down stairs hysterical but tumbled to the bottom. We looked at her and noticed the bullet in her head. The guys looked behind them and saw an array of niggas with lasers.

"Is this her?" K asked walking closer to the dark-skinned chick, whose name I still didn't know. I nodded. K circled her and smirked.

"Leave her out of it." The guy yelled out that she kissed. Him and the rest of the guys were all on their knees with hands behind their heads.

"Why should I do that? You didn't think to leave her out trying to set my people's up."

"Fuck you." The chick shouted and stood by the guy.

"If this is your girl, you really should've told her about us."

*PHEW! PHEW!*

K shot her twice in the head. Her body hit the floor and dude tried to jump up. Misfit damn near beat the shit out him. Him and K are best friends and we were all family, regardless if our parents weren't the same. I'm very protective of my family but Misfit is a psychopath.

"That's enough Misfit." He backed away after kicking him in the face one last time. K nodded and everyone of the men were laid out on the ground.

"I want flowers sent to all of their homes and I specifically want a dozen black ones sent to B-huff. He knows better than to come for us."

"How do you know it was him?" Champ asked going through the guys pockets. He got all of their license and he liked to take everything niggas had. His ass always did crazy shit.

"The one running his mouth about the chick, is his cousin. He came to help him run the business."

"Damn." I said and walked with K outside.

"You niggas have to do better. Strippers bro." I shrugged my shoulders.

"When are you going to settle down and give mommy grand babies?"

"As soon as there's no more strip clubs and all the woman let themselves go and look like shit." We busted out laughing.

"I'm serious."

"So am I." K walked away and into the awaiting car. I knew my pops was going to hear about this shit because of the war K just started. Oh well, I didn't want to be in this shit from the beginning.

\*\*\*\*\*\*\*\*\*\*\*\*\*\*\*\*

"Son you have to do better." My pops said handing me a drink. I knew he was speaking of what went down with the strippers and the dudes B-Huff sent to kill us.

"I didn't think he would hire strippers to help but I guess no bitch is exempt."

"No, they're not. Do you think my wife, your mother would fall for a man putting her in a position to die like that?"

266

"No."

"Exactly, so while you saw those women as strippers, they were actually some of his best hit women and so were the guys. Luckily, you were able to contact K in time to come help you out. Now I'm not saying you're a slouch but what if K didn't make it in time or what would've happened if they did kill you?" I put my head down. My father always had a way of making you think about shit.

"I get it pops."

"Do you Shafee?"

"I said yea." I stood up and he did the same.

"Don't ever step in a motherfucker's face if you're not ready for the consequences." I knew him saying that meant he was ready to swing off.

See my dad is a retired savage slash kingpin. He is still feared by many to this very day and the successor, who is K, is just as ruthless as him. People knew of K, but like my father, K stayed out of the spotlight. No one on the streets could describe K to you. It's as if K is a ghost and for now it needs to stay that way.

"Get the fuck out my house and make sure you don't do no more reckless shit like that again. Got your mother worried about you all the time and when she worries, then I do." I blew my breath listening to him go on and on about the same shit.

"Take some money out and invest in a business because you've become very lazy lately and no kid of mine will be living scott free." I didn't bother going back and forth with him. I may not work but he damn sure knows, I put in work, in other areas when needed.

I hopped in my car and drove home. I picked my phone up and called one of my many hoes to come break me off. Hopefully, it will hold me over until I find me some new pussy.

# Misfit Holden

"Stop it daddy, you're going to make me tinkle on myself." My seven-year-old daughter Angel said, as I tickled her stomach.

"You better not or I'm going to tell your friends."

"Daddy no." She was lying on her back in the bed trying to get away.

"Misfit, leave my grand baby alone. It's bad enough she barely listens to anyone as it is."

"Ma, what does me tickling her have to do with listening?"

"Give it a second." I stopped tickling her.

"Angel, can you go get nana a glass of soda? I need to talk to daddy for a minute?" She instantly folded her arms across her chest and sat there.

"Angel did you hear nana?"

"Yea but I don't want to. She is old enough to.-" I popped her ass right in the mouth. It wasn't hard but enough to let her know the shit coming out her mouth won't be tolerated.

"Roll your eyes again and see what happens. Now go do what she asked." She hopped off the bed and stormed passed my mom.

"I told you." I waved my mom off but I knew she was right. Angel is the replica of her mother and has the attitude to match.

"What up ma?" I sat there waiting for her to speak.

"I wanted to tell you, I'm moving into my own place and before you object, don't. I'm only forty-six and I'll be damned if I stay celibate because your bratty ass wants me close." I had to laugh because my mom wanted some D and she knew wasn't no man coming in here.

"Ma, if you want sex why don't you rent a room?"

"Why would I do that, when I can have my own place? What if I want him to sleep over? Wait a minute, why am I explaining myself? I'm the parent. You heard what I said."

"Alright ma, damn."

"Boy you better watch your mouth." She popped me on the back of the head and walked out, only to be stopped by Angel.

"Here you go nana." She handed her the soda.

"Thanks baby but I'm not thirsty anymore."

"That's why I didn't want to get it for you. You always do that."

"Angel Rose Holden, apologize right now before I beat your ass." I heard my baby mom Unique saying.

"I'm sorry nana. I just hate doing things and then you change your mind."

"Oh, you mean like how we go out to eat and I have to buy you different food after you tried one thing and didn't like it? Or when we go shopping and I'm sitting there while you try on different shoes or clothes."

"Oh, that's different nana. I'm a kid and you're supposed to do that." My mom sucked her teeth and walked out.

"Angel go with nana, while I talk to daddy." Unique closed the door and came over to where I sat on the bed.

"What up?" I stared at Unique for a minute and for a second wanted her back in my life but it quickly changed when I noticed her texting on the phone. She's not with anyone but it always bothered me when she wanted to talk and would entertain her phone instead.

Unique is the only woman I ever loved to this day but we couldn't be together. She was half Spanish and black, with long black hair that went to the middle of her back. She wasn't real thick but enough to be called it. The sex with her is off the chain and she has my daughter, who is also the love of my life.

272

The reason we can't be together is one... like most men; I cheated on her a few times. She almost killed me after the last time and two... I wasn't and I'm still not ready to settle down. For the record, me cheating on Unique had nothing to do with her not handling me correctly. Shit, I'm a man who loves to party and if a woman offers me sex, as long as I have a condom, she's getting fucked. Is it right no, but it is what it is?

All men have that one special woman in their life; Unique is that woman for me. She can have whatever she wants and no chick will ever come before her. If she needs me, I'm there without a second thought. This woman is my best friend now and we would never do anything to destroy that. As far as I know, she has the same feeling towards me.

"I want to have a party for my birthday."

"Ok, so why you telling me? You know I'll be there." I laid back on the bed and she climbed on top of me. The crazy part about it is, we did this all the time. If she wanted my full attention she needed to be in my face and I do the same.

"Misfittttttt." She whined and sat up on my lap.

"Down boy." She said and moved over on the bed. That's the only problem with us being this close. It's been two years and we haven't slept together but the attraction is still there.

"You know when you sit up like that he wakes up. What's up though? Why you whining?" I sat up and she laid her head on my lap.

"I want you to throw it."

"Unique you bugging. I don't know how to throw no chick party except Angel's and you do most of that."

"Well figure it out because I want one." She got off the bed and walked to the door. Angel little ass wanted to come in.

"Who you bossing up on?"

"My baby daddy."

"Stop calling me that." She opened the door and my daughter came strolling in with her hands on her hips.

"What took you so long to open it?" She gave Unique a hard stare.

"First of all little girl.-"

"Don't even think about it Unique. All she did was ask a question." Angel sat by me and thought I didn't notice that smirk on her face. Unique came closer.

"Remember that, when you want me to have phone sex with your ass again." She whispered and left the room.

Yea, we don't sleep with one another but we'll have phone sex like a motherfucker. However, we both made a vow that when we were serious about someone we'd stop but hell, neither of us had anyone, so her ass better answer tonight when I call, because it's definitely on.

\*\*\*\*\*\*\*\*\*\*\*\*\*\*\*\*\*\*

"Man, good luck throwing the party for her." Shafee said about his sister Unique. He knew as well as I, that she is hard to please when it comes to certain things. However, he knew I'd get it done.

"Excuse me sir. Would you like me to refill your drink?" Some chick asked behind me.

"Did I ask for a drink?" I barked at her without turning around.

"Hold on nigga. It's my job to ask if your glass is either half empty or unfilled. A simple no would've been fine." I turned around and she was pretty as hell. Her skin was a dark mocha color and she had on some high waisted shorts that showed her long legs. She had on minimal makeup, her body was petite but she had a nice ass.

"Who you talking to?"

"I'm talking to you. Fix that fucking attitude before you bring your nappy headed ass out in public." She said and stormed off. Shafee and Champ were hysterical laughing, where I didn't find shit funny.

"Leave it alone man." Champ stood in front of me.

"Nah fuck her. She needs to know who the.-"

"I don't need to know shit. Fuck you." She had her purse and phone in her hand as she moved past.

Champ wouldn't allow me to go after her but I know for a fact I'm going to run into her ass again. I want to see if she'll be singing the same tune when I have her ass yoked the hell up. I slammed my drink down and told my boys I'd see them later. All these drinks had my ass horny and I needed a release.

Instead of hitting up one of my freaks, I called up the only one I knew could get me where I needed without touching her. I dialed the number on my way home and waited for her to pick up. I thought about the last time we had sex.

*"I missed you today." She said when I walked in the house. We were living separately and she was my peace every*

277

time I made it over here. I tore her nightgown off and carried her in the bedroom.

"Misfit, I'm cumming baby. Fuckkkkk yesssss." Her legs trembled and I continued pleasing her until she had a few more. In return, she gave me the same pleasure. I laid behind her with my arm wrapped around her.

"I love you Unique. You know that right?"

"I do and feel the same but you know we have to stop this." She turned over to face me.

"I know but you're the only woman whose pussy I enjoy the most."

"And you're the only man whose had his dick in me without strapping up. The only man who has ever had me. And the only one who hurt me. Misfit look." She sat up.

"I love you with everything in me and if I thought for a minute you could settle down and be with only me, I would be with you. Baby, we're both young and it's a lot of temptation

*out there. I'm not as angry as I used to be but this can't go on."*
*She stroked my dick back to life with her hand and in one swift*
*motion guided herself down on me.*

*"Got damn you feel so good." She threw her head back*
*and went in circles.*

*"Misfit, it's been years and I still love this dick.*
*Fuckkkkk baby. Make love to me one last time. Shit." She*
*moaned out and leaned towards me for a kiss.*

*"What are you saying?" We've been together since she*
*was seventeen and now she's breaking up with me.*

*"After tonight, there will be no more us. We have to*
*move on and we can't if we're still pleasing each other." She*
*squeezed her muscles together and my ass came in her womb.*

*"I'm not letting you go Unique."*

*"Misfit, please. You know like I do, that it's what's best.*
*We have a beautiful daughter and we'll always be connected."*
*I stared at her as she sat on top of me crying.*

279

*I know I hurt her in the past but I didn't think she'd ever put a stop to us having sex. I wanted to fight for her but I also knew I wouldn't do right and after the last time I cheated, she took it hard and I don't want to see her like that again. I pulled her face close to mine and kissed her.*

*"Well if this is my last time, I'm about to make that pussy talk." She wrapped her arms around my neck and the two of us gave each other multiple pleasures throughout the night.*

*"I love you Unique and I'll always be here." I whispered in her ear as she slept.*

*I stood up to get dressed and stared at her. I can't believe we took it there but I'm glad she gave me one last time to make love to her. I would give my life for her but she's right, we'll never be with anyone if we don't leave the other alone. I grabbed my things and made my way out the door. That was two years ago and the closest I got to her pussy is over the phone through face time.*

"Hello." She answered and brought me out of my thoughts. I closed my bedroom door and locked it.

"Damn Unique that pussy looks real good." She already had her legs spread open as if she were waiting for me.

The two of us talked shit and had each other cumming but we both knew this is as far as we'd take it. We hung the phone up and I took my ass to sleep. Maybe it is time for me to look elsewhere because if I can't have Unique, I may as well grow old with someone else.

## *Coming Soon!!!!!*

Made in the USA
Columbia, SC
12 June 2018